Chasing AZRA

Matthew Curcio

D1607576

Chasing Azra: Introduction
March 2023

The one thing we all have in common is that we need a job after college, at least to start.

He couldn't have been a day over twenty-two. His face screamed entry-level college graduate, and that's exactly what I was looking for.

"Nicholas, do you go by Nick or Nicky?"

"I actually go by Cal."

"Oh, I see your last name is Caliola? Must be Italian?"

"It's 2023, you shouldn't make assumptions like that," Nicholas told me.

We both went silent, and I stared down at Nicholas's resume.

"You're right, I apologize."

"I'm totally kidding, I was just trying to lighten the mood."

I was relieved; the last thing I needed was bad PR to start my new company.

"Well, sounds like you got a good sense of humor. I like that. I also like that you studied Finance at Baruch with a double major in Marketing as well."

"That's correct, I had to prepare myself. The world's changing. As you know, everything's super digital. The NFTs, the metaverse, all that jazz."

Cal was a sharp kid. I had to have him, but I didn't want to reveal too much. I also didn't have any leverage, so I was stuck between a rock and a hard place.

"I couldn't agree more. I also have to ask, how'd you hear about me?"

Cal pointed to the framed Forbes article that hung above the only two desks in the space. My claim to fame.

"Well, Max, I figured you have to be somewhat legit if Forbes wrote an article on you?"

"I like to think so. But I'm going to be honest, I can't offer you much. Low base pay, but you will have solid benefits. Health, Dental, Vision. 401k, no match, though, sorry."

"That sounds great. How about equity?"

"Good question. Well, there's something to be said about timing. After ninety days of employment, should you accept, I'll offer one percent of the company. How's that sound?"

"You would be willing to give up one percent to me?"

"Now, don't go screwing it up. Listen, you're going to be the human resources coordinator, social media manager, podcast co-host, and sales guy. Boots on the ground heavy, in the trenches, it's going to be a lot. I can do $50,000 a year, but we can also get you a solid commission structure with extra incentives."

"This sounds incredible. But can I ask you something?" Cal asked.

"Sure, anything. What is it, Cal?"

"What's your story, Max? How did you end up here? I read up on your background, and it sounds like you made a big leap. I guess what I'm asking is, why would I want to work with you, Max? I can call you Max, right?"

Dedicated to: New York City
"The Good & The Bad"

March 1, 2020	**First COVID-19 case in New York State**
March 7, 2020	NY Governor Andrew Cuomo declares a state of emergency
March 8, 2020	NYC issues guidelines to avoid densely packed buses, subways, or trains
March 10, 2020	Governor Cuomo orders containment zone in New Rochelle from March 12 to 25
March 12, 2020	Events with more than 500 people must be cancelled or postponed
March 12, 2020	Broadway shuts down
March 13, 2020	President Trump declares a national emergency
March 14, 2020	**First two COVID-19 deaths in NYS**
March 15, 2020	C.D.C. recommendeds no gatherings of 50+ in the U.S.
March 16, 2020	**NYC public schools close**
March 17, 2020	**NYC bars and restaurants close, except for delivery**
March 22, 2020	**NYS on Pause Program begins, all non-essential workers must stay home**
March 27, 2020	President signs the CARES Act
March 27, 2020	U.S. reaches the most COVID-19 cases in the world
March 28, 2020	**Governor Cuomo halts all nonessential construction sites in NYS**
March 30, 2020	USNS Comfort arrives in NYC
March 31, 2020	NYC passes 1,000 COVID-19 deaths

February 2020

Chapter 1: The World of Finance

I can still remember how my iced coffee sat on the already soggy napkin that held my can of Pepsi like a coaster from the night before. I looked at the two men in black suits who were paid a competitive salary to "stay alert" and secure the workplace's property. I was no law enforcement agent, nor did I have a background in loss prevention, but I could see the pair of corporate security guards make an unusual movement towards the glass doors that welcomed the public to the midtown office of our private equity fund. They were probably 47 or 48 years of age at most, and one always arched his back—maybe he got hurt at some point on the job. The other still believed he was part of the secret service or whatever federal agency he had served, with the way he adjusted his American flag lapel pin. The wire that ran down each of their necks vibrated just enough to tell me something was going on. They constantly kept their heads on a swivel, not because it was necessary but due to instinct. Soon, they began to walk towards my desk. This was around the same time my company laptop lit up with an incoming message on our internal communications platform.

"Mr. Yates, got a minute?" my boss asked.

He was not just my boss; he was my mentor, our company president, and the founder of the small, local, boutique fund that had seen better days with higher returns and much fatter holiday bonuses. He was also the man that welcomed me into the hustle and grind that encompassed the greed of NYC finance.

"Be there in a second."

It was around that time the two security guards came my way. They timed it out perfectly to let me walk on my own, but I knew what was happening.

"Hey, Colt, you wanted to talk to me?" My knuckles double-tapped the plexiglass that had his name spelled out in a bold and professional font. *Braxen Equity Associates, Established 2003.*

His real name was *Jed Braxenhultz*. We called him "Colt" because he hadn't missed a home NFL game in Indianapolis since 1998. The framed Peyton Manning jersey sat in the upper right corner of his office, the stubs to the Super Bowl tickets displayed just below next to the replica souvenir football that he probably received from his wife on Christmas a year after.

"Maximo, take a seat," Colt instructed.

The two retired law enforcement officers, now rent-a-cops, folded their hands as I looked back at them. I looked at the guards and smiled to reassure them that I was not going to resist or cause a scene once this was all over.

"This Covid-19 thing," Colt started as he held back emotion. "I would not be surprised if the pandemic destroys this firm."

"I mean, Colt, c'mon, you said if I got my MBA, my position would be safe for the future?"

"I know what I said, okay? But technically you're still the youngest full-time associate at the firm. I'm no spring chicken, okay? My daughters are going to disown me if this company shuts its doors. Now, I need to make cutbacks. It's nothing personal."

"This is my career we're talking about," I said, looking back at the security guards. "Can I just get five minutes?" I tried to control my frustration as I adjusted my collar and flattened out my hair.

The guards both patted me on the shoulder and honored my request.

"Be right over here If you need us, boss," the shorter, chubbier one said as he exited the cubed enclosure.

"Look, I am so sorry," Colt said as he rubbed his hands on his face—something the CDC (Center for Disease Control) strongly advised against.

"You know you're fucking me over, right? Also, what does some random virus have to do with our firm?"

"I know.

"Those fucking Harvard business school interns. You're going to keep them, aren't you? You had me train them quick just for that. You're a fucking asshole."

"Listen, in the four or so years you were here, did I ever lie to you or promise anything I couldn't back up? Did I?"

"Colt, I get it. But loyalty?"

"I know, you're right." Colt grabbed his coffee and wrapped his index fingers together.

"I rent a luxury studio a hundred yards from the Freedom Tower. How am I supposed to pay rent?"

"I know, Max," Colt said. He avoided eye contact, understandably

"I have most of my money tied up in stocks and mutual funds. I have more than a few bucks in student loan debt because you told me you could only pay for sixty-five percent of my graduate school education. I would have gone to Baruch, but you insisted on Columbia."

"I know, and I'm proud you did it the right way. You'll be fine. After all, you now have the Ivy League logo under your belt."

"Where are *your* prestigious degrees? What, Indiana? Kelley School of Business? Before the Ivy League degree, I was a product of the Stern School. I'm more qualified to work here than you are, apparently."

"Why don't I do this? Thirty-thousand dollars and full pay for three months. You're like a son to me—the one I never had. You think I'm going to just let you rot, collect unemployment, and then feed you to the birds?"

As bad as I felt and as angry as I was, I knew that in some ways, it was a solid deal.

"Thirty-thousand dollars along with three months full pay? You sure you can deliver on that?"

"Yes, Max. You've earned that from me."

"I'm not happy, for the record."

"Well, I would like you to at least consider returning after I get back on my feet. Give me some time?"

12

"I don't think so. Have you ever gone through a break-up? From the family photos I've seen, I would assume not. It's very rare to run back to the person who left you stranded in the desert with thirty-thousand dollars but no water; we both know that in the desert, that money is only half a glass of Poland Spring. Just enough to make you forget how thirsty you are."

"I know, but I have to do this. People are dying, companies are shifting work to the home office. They're saying Covid-19 is the real thing. Our safety and health should be our most important focus, at least for now."

"Alright, I'll ship any equipment back to Andre, and I'll CC your assistant Melissa. I'm sure Melissa will still have a job, right? That associate degree and big smile... You wouldn't get rid of her, would you?" I said, sticking out my palm that had a classy yet simplistic Rolex watch that served as a reminder of who I was: the son of a lawyer.

Security proceeded to guide me out. But as licensed guards in New York State, they had little to no authority, and I took full advantage of that.

"If one of you lays a hand on me, I'll make it a personal mission to ensure that none of you ever work in corporate security again."

The guards guided me to the first floor via the elevator. Their silence was a reminder of their experience. They never folded; it was just another day at the office.

"Use this time to go find yourself, kid. It's a shitty situation, but you are young enough to rebound. It will be like this never happened."

I nodded but still tried to maintain the stern look that controlled my expression.

"You two take care."

I then began my journey through the lunch rush of midtown. It was a warm afternoon, so instead of the subway, I chose to walk. Instead of the healthy salad and Fiji water that my ex-firm provided for lunch, I decided to break the rules of my diet. I bought a hotdog and a cold soda (I didn't count my Pepsi obsession). I didn't care if I spilled some ketchup on my crisp white Brooks Brothers Oxford shirt with brown buttons that contrasted the base of my button-down. It did me right to get messy. I had to cut myself some slack and let go of the stress of Manhattan along with the pressure of the rat race that came along with finance in the biggest city in the country. I loosened the cap and took a deep chug of my soda. The reality of my situation had yet to sink in, so I decided to call my parents and face the music. I took out my phone and scrolled through my recent calls. If I was going to rip the band-aid off, I was going to tear it with my eyes closed.

"Hey, Mom, can you put Dad on?"

My mom was like my best friend, but I always went to my dad for advice. My mom could smell an emergency from miles away, and she knew I would have texted first if anything was seriously wrong. She put my dad on without saying more than a few words.

"Max?"

"Hey, Dad. Uh, listen. Well, there is no easy way to say this, but Colt just let me go from the firm. By the way, this isn't a joke or a prank. I'm being very serious."

"When?"

"Less than an hour ago. I know, I can't believe it either."

"Well, did you do something wrong?"

"It's Covid-19 related. Budget, you know, that ugly type of stuff. I don't know, maybe it's not the worst thing. This so-called pandemic sounds pretty serious."

"Oh, son, I'm so sorry. That's too bad." He sounded ashamed, as to be expected.

"He did offer me thirty-thousand dollars as an exit bonus and three months full pay as severance."

"Oh, well, that's amazing. We should celebrate. You should go meet up with friends and grab a drink."

"No, Dad, I just got fired. I need to start looking for a new job."

"No, you don't. Not right away, at least. Your exit bonus is more than your mother makes all year. You can use that money to figure out what you will do next."

My father was and still is a prestigious lawyer in the political center of Washington D.C. When I was a senior in high school, he opened his practice. My mom works at a nail salon in town just to keep busy. She never took things personally, but I could hear her voice in the background, "That's not nice, Allen."

"What do you think I should do?"

"Listen, son, you have two degrees. You're smart, funny, the list goes on."

15

"Not smart enough to keep my job."

"I think you're better than that place. Take some time off, maybe clear your head. By the way, your mother wants you to stay safe. She told me to tell you to buy a mask. It's funny you bring up Covid-19; I've been working from home for weeks now. I never realized how great of a cook your mother is."

"It's nothing. It's going to pass," I reminded my father with optimism.

"We hope so. Oh, another thing; your mother went into your room and found an old note from Azra. Do you still keep in touch with her?"

I took the last bite of my hot dog and washed it down with Pepsi before my stomach sank to pieces. "Mom found a note from Azra?"

"Yeah, earlier today. She didn't read it, don't worry; she was just doing some early spring cleaning. Have you two spoken recently?"

"Dad, I told you, she moved back to Turkey after nursing school."

"Seems a little odd to move home to Istanbul to become a nurse when she attended school here in the states, but okay…whatever you say. I guess your mom got nostalgic thinking about her."

"I wish I got closure on her, too, Dad, but like you always said, life's not always fair."

"You're right, son. I'm proud of you for staying tough. I didn't mean to upset you with the whole Azra thing, I won't bring it up again."

"Okay, Dad. Well, I have to run. I'll talk to you later"

"Call me tomorrow. I'll go over any legal documents your boss sends over for you to sign. It's most likely a standard severance package, but I'll redline it just to be safe. Talk soon."

Chapter 2: College

Fall 2011

Azra was my college girlfriend. We met in the late summer/early fall semester of 2011 during our NYU men versus women-friendly scrimmage. I was on the men's varsity team, and she was a member of the women's varsity squad. It was a beautiful story, how we met—maybe too perfect for those who read poetry and romance novels.

It was a "no contact" exhibition match. We were ordered and briefed by coaches to not play physically minded. The rules were simple, silly things like avoiding slide tackles and other potentially dangerous encroachment. But in the first five minutes, Azra dribbled into the box to take a shot. I was coming from the middle of the pitch and could not resist arguably the best part of playing defense. So, I slid and stole the ball right from under her feet. I figured the coaches would let it go, but Azra laid there in agony, screaming and begging for the pain to subside. I continued to run until my teammates pointed and whistled behind me, convincing me to turn around. I saw Azra pounding the turf with her fists. The head women's coach ran over quickly with student trainers and support staff.

My coach grabbed me by the arm and sat my ass on the bench. "You'll be lucky if you make it to *week one* after the stunt you just pulled."

There was absolutely no doubt Azra was seriously injured. It would be a miracle if she walked off the field on her terms. So, I prayed to myself for a few seconds and then got up and faced Azra and her teammates.

"Hey, I was wrong for that, for the record, I am so sorry," I told her.

"Fuck you, you narcissistic piece of shit."

And it was at that moment I fell in love. For the rest of the scrimmage, I held ice on her leg as she lay down on a sturdy but forty-year-old NYC park bench, her hands buried in her eyes. Eventually, she spoke up, as her silence was not enough for the moment. She stared at me and shook her head like I was a pretty boy who had just received detention for the first time in his life and she was the disappointed teacher.

"I'm still very mad at you," Azra said as she let her arms hang from the antique, city-mandated pine.

"I'm Max," I said. I stuck my hand out like it was a peace treaty waiting to be signed.

"Azra, as you probably heard."

"That's a beautiful name."

"Don't suck up. I'm still upset, but it was a nice slide tackle, if we're being honest."

We shared a laugh. Azra was clearly in considerable pain, but she was flirting with me! Who knew I could be so charming during my darkest hour?

"Thanks, that makes me feel better."

"Okay, cut the shit. I told you it was a nice tackle, no need to grovel any further. I can't blame you though; you're probably just trying to show your skills on the team. You're a D1 talent, D2 at the very least. What are you doing here?"

I started to blush; I had a few offers to play D1 ball out west. "I suppose I could play at a higher level."

"And?" Azra said as she lifted her ice.

"Well, my grades weren't quite good enough for Columbia, so NYU was the next best thing. Plus, I like the cold weather. I don't do well with too much sun."

"Was it New York or nowhere?"

"Oh yeah, ever since I was nine, that's always been the plan. My dad took me to an exhibition game, I think it was Manchester United against some random US select team. It didn't matter who was playing, all that mattered was that we got to come to New York City."

"That's when you knew?"

Azra was wincing in pain, but her effort to stay in tune with the conversation was something to be admired.

"I still remember driving in and seeing the skyline from a distance. There was nothing like it. That's when I knew."

"That's sweet," Azra said. "Ah, ah, ah, ah! This is starting to hurt," she cried out.

"Let me hold this." I reached out and grabbed the ice pack, placing it a little further north on her ankle.

"That feels better. Keep it right there."

"Is that good?"

"That's perfect. So now it's your turn to ask me."

"Ask you what?" I had known college girls to be complicated but never this complex.

"Ask me why I wanted to study in New York City?"

I closed my eyes and held in my laugh as the August sun gently hit the corner of my forehead, just below my hairline. "So why did you want to study in New York City, Azra?"

"Glad you asked. Well, my dad's a pilot for Turkish Airlines. He's kind of my superhero." Azra smiled. "Anyway, one day, we took a trip, just him and me, and I can still remember flying over those tall buildings, each one so perfectly distant yet so magically close."

"The city that never sleeps," I said.

"It never rests. Never, not for anybody."

"I think that's why I ultimately decided on New York; anything can happen here. The city, to me, is like a game. One move this way, and who knows? Things can change forever. Kind of like soccer, right?"

"Go on." Azra threatened me with her ice pack. She used it as a weapon, but the cold water from the plastic was refreshing and soothing, more like a bandage for my recent guilty act.

"Well, I don't know about you, Azra, but most games growing up were close matches, at least for me."

"There are typically only a few goals scored each game."

"Exactly," I said. "I play defense for one reason, and that's because, for my whole life, I felt like I had something to protect. But in soccer, you could play a great game for 89 minutes, and at the very last second, you slip, and someone shoots and scores and wins the game."

"I like where this is going," Azra told me. "Almost like in New York, the opportunity is everywhere but it almost always comes at a cost."

"Yes, very much so. Take my slide tackle, for example. If I hesitate, you score, and maybe we never meet. But, on the other hand, I tackle you, and suddenly, I'm talking to the prettiest girl on the squad. Who would have thought?"

Azra stood up on the bench as if suddenly her ankle had begun to heal magically. "You know you're smooth, don't you?"

"Smooth is one way to put it. Nobody growing up wanted to play defense; they always said it was boring. In my opinion, playing defense is the only way I know how to score."

"That's an interesting perspective," Azra said.

For a moment, time stopped, and all I could do was look at this beautiful girl, who was beginning to feel less and less like a stranger. Her hair was silky smooth despite the sweat and warm weather. Her lips were thick, the perfect type of round. Her complexion reminded me of an expensive doll in the window of a boutique store, hung like a wooden marionette. Her eyes—oh, her eyes were the best part of her being. Her brown pupils were bold, complemented by the lashes that hung above them like a black awning in summer. Her voice echoed tough, but it was also sweet at times when she changed her cadence and adjusted her mood. She also had breasts that were perfectly fit for her stature. Growing up, most female soccer players I knew were tall and skinny, but Azra was tiny, athletic, and in perfect shape. Her hips were extensive but not too vast, and her legs stood proportionally with the rest of her frame. Her personality was the cherry on top of her natural appearance, and her skill on the pitch was good—not above my prowess, but above average.

"Well, I hope you don't have a jealous girlfriend back home or something?"

"Oh, none of the girls back home in D.C. were worth my time."

"Good, because you're going to be buying me dinner and carrying my books for the next few weeks."

"At least something positive will come from my dirty deed, I suppose? Plus, I'll be the first guy on campus to take you out." I held my fist out for a pound but would have settled for a high five at that moment.

"Is that how Americans do it?"

"Yeah, you've never given a pound? You know, pound it?" I opened my fist like a volcano explosion. "You know, whoosh?"

"You Americans are corny, you know that?"

"Oh, I've got a lot to teach you," I told her.

"You move fast, you know that?"

"Slow down, Azra, we just met."

"I can already tell that you're nothing but trouble, but I do like it. You're a bad boy, but a nice boy."

We stayed on the bench together for a few more minutes. A knot formed in my stomach. I recognized a feeling that I only had once or twice before, still, never this deep. That emotion when someone provides a sense of comfortability despite not knowing everything there is to learn. The mystery is so suspenseful, so inviting.

Eventually, additional support staff arrived to check on Azra.

"He got you pretty good?" the head trainer asked. The full-time physical therapist, converted to a college trainer, began to cover her ankle in pink "pre-wrap," as Azra looked on.

"It's not Max's fault; it was a clean tackle if I've ever seen one."

My coach began to wander over. "So, what do you think is the appropriate punishment for Max? Sprints, 6:00 a.m. stairs workouts, you name it."

"Just play him…but play him all ninety minutes."

Azra and I were still practically strangers, but even she could tell that I wasn't attending NYU for soccer. Azra knew that I would have much rather enjoyed exploring the city as opposed to perfecting a child's game that she and I both knew would never be a part of our long-term future.

"So, you're telling me to start him?"

"Make him play hard, then he and I are even."

I nodded at Azra. Getting kicked off the team would have been far from ideal, and her support was appreciated.

"Well, you're in luck. It looks like a bad bruise—which doesn't mean you'll be back in ten days; this is going to take a few weeks of recovery."

"Thank God," I said under my breath.

"You dodged one. You better start running if you want to stick around for the whole game. Walk your new friend to the team bus; I will have an assistant drive you back."

Azra put her arm on my waist. I sucked in my stomach and flexed my abs so she would feel some muscle. One of the graduate team managers drove us back to the dorms, and that ride was something I would cherish forever. Azra elevated her ankle on my waist for the whole trip. We both stared out the window. We were on the same page as our eyes followed the stories of hundreds of New Yorkers. The horns of cab drivers played like theme songs, and sirens of ambulances bolted down crowded avenues and side streets. Kids ran up the blocks as mothers juggled ice cream cones and soda, chasing after their kin. It felt like we were on a road trip. The backseat was warm, the leather beaten up over years of wear and tear, but it was toasty. There was no denying the comfort. The Yankee game played on the radio. It was already 4:00 P.M., but it was New York City in the summer, so the day was getting started.

We finally got out of the sprinter van, and Azra grabbed my shoulders as we hobbled out together as one.

"How's it feeling?" I asked.

"Eh, I was a little dramatic at practice. I'm not sure if you can tell, Max, but I could give two hoots about playing college soccer."

"Well, at least we're on the same page."

"But this," Azra yelled out. She spread her arms wide and lifted her shoulders together in the sky. "This right here is what it's all about."

"Quite beautiful at this time of day, wouldn't you agree?" I asked.

"It is. But I'm hungry. Do you like Turkish food, Max?"

"I've never had it."

There was something about Azra's presence that made me feel comfortable being transparent. Most guys would have lied and told Azra about their travels through Eastern Europe. But that was the beauty of Manhattan. You could try new things, but more importantly, you could open up to strangers.

"Oh, Max, you're in for a real treat."

"Done, let's get to it," I said.

"Awesome. Let me just put on something more comfortable and drop off my bag. Here, let me take yours, if you don't mind."

I handed my bag to Azra, knowing very well I was going to have to come over and grab it after dinner. Her eyes lit up, as did mine.

"Just give me a few minutes," she told me.

I waited outside her dorm and clenched my fist like Tiger Woods winning at the 18th hole of Augusta. It was already the best day of my life. I could not wait to tell my teammates, and I couldn't wait for Azra to come back down. I prayed this wasn't some sort of prank.

"Okay, ready?" Azra said. This time, her crutches guided her out to the street.

"Where'd you get the crutches? That was fast."

"Don't worry about it."

Dinner went as smoothly as it could have gone. Our first date was magical. I mean, Doner

Kebab (Turkish Gyro), of all meals. Whoever thought European cuisine could taste that good. But ultimately, my fate lay in the dessert. My bag was in her room. Technically, I didn't have to grab it; I could have let it sit and pick it up tomorrow. But even as a naive eighteen-year-old, I knew I had to step up to the plate.

"So, what are you going to do for the rest of the night?"

"I don't know, maybe just Xbox with the guys. Nothing too crazy. Just relax. How about you?"

"Same thing, minus the Xbox, of course. My roommate, Megan, tried out for the team but ended up getting cut. I chose to room with her, assuming we would both be playing, but she's great—it worked out well."

"Oh, cool, and where is she from?"

"Michigan, outside of Detroit."

"Oh, wow, far away from home, huh?"

"I mean, she's living with someone from Istanbul, so Detroit must feel like a hop and a skip away."

At this point, we were just filling in conversation. It was what they called in Sociology 101 a "Cliché Convo."

"So, I think I left my bag at your place. You took it up to your room?"

"That I did. You know what, Max, you should stop by and come grab it. Megan made brownies."

"That sounds amazing. I'm in."

"Let me just run to the restroom and then we can go back!"

Azra stood up and grabbed her crutches. Her walk through the alley of small tables and chairs seemed to last an eternity. Azra was tough, but sweet when she had to be. I learned this from observing how she said, "Excuse me," as she made her way between the remaining customers. I nervously opened my phone and scrolled through old photos, doing anything to kill the remaining minutes. I whistled and felt my anxiety approaching. Now I had to go to the bathroom.

"I suppose I can just wait until I reach her dorm," I said out loud. "Screw it," I reiterated. I rushed to the bathroom in hopes of beating Azra, but she met me halfway.

"Where are you going?"

"I just realized I have to use the bathroom, too. I'll be super quick."

"Take your time, there's no rush. We have all night."

My face turned hot red. *Do we have all night?* That's a phrase you hear when you spend the night, or at least that's how it is in the movies. I took the longest stretch of urination in my eighteen years of living. "C'mon, c'mon, c'mon hurry up."

I finished up and made my way back to the table. The only thing was, Azra was no longer there.

"Azra?" I yelled.

A part of me thought she had left; maybe she was nervous, too. But as soon as I pushed the metal barrier that held the reversible "open/close" sign, I saw her against the glass window with a newly lit cigarette. The smoke inhaled quickly into her lungs and her lips tasted the tobacco as we locked eyes.

"Smoke?" she asked.

"I don't, but smoke 'em if you got 'em."

"I've never heard that before, but I like it."

"It's an old WWII phrase. I learned it from my grandfather."

I held my hand over the lighter like I had smoked a million times before. I took my first inhalation, and it was a complete mess. I started coughing uncontrollably.

"Well, I might steal it from the American soldiers," Azra said.

I began to regain some strength in my lungs, and my chest began to clench. "He used to tell me all these life lessons and stories from the war. He was part of the capturing of Nazis throughout various parts of Europe during the Holocaust"

"Oh wow, I want to hear more."

"Yeah, it's pretty crazy. I never thought of my grandfather as a hero. He was a funny guy. Liked to laugh. He made my grandmother happy." I looked down. "That's all I thought of him."

"Oh no, I noticed you said he *was*? Did he recently pass?"

"Yes, just of old age. Nothing sad, nothing that would make you say, *Oh that's terrible, I'm sorry.*"

"And how about your grandmother?"

"Three months later. My dad went to check on her, and she just passed into the night. She had my grandfather's picture clenched in her right palm, the rosary draped over her arms."

"Wait, that's adorable. I want to cry. Now see, that right there, *that's* the sad part of this life we live. I'm sorry."

"They say it's possible to die of a broken heart. Do you believe that?"

Azra took a heavy breath, dropping her cigarette to the side. "Very much so."

"Before my grandfather passed, I was with him for his last couple of days. He said, 'Max, when I'm gone, I'll still be here. Technically, I'll be gone, but I'll send you signs.'"

"Have you seen any from him recently?" Azra asked. "You mind if I light another? I'm enjoying this conversation."

"I'm seeing one right now," I told her. I pointed across the street at the narrow park that was large enough for about three park benches, although the Department of Parks and Recreation had insisted they squeeze in five. A shadow of a man, dimmed by a broken streetlight, played music softly, the tune unrecognizable.

"Yeah, violin, did he play?"

"Oh, you bet he played," I told her. "I'll take another cigarette, by the way."

Azra opened her pack, and I grabbed a fresh cig.

"That's the most amazing thing I've heard since I landed here."

"He learned from a couple at Flossenburg—one of the main concentration camps in Germany. He told me that it was an instruction from the musical gods to keep going."

"How did he meet your grandmother?"

"His first day back in the states."

"Oh, this is a true love story."

"My grandmother worked at a veterans post-war employment agency. She was trying to get him a job at the post office or the police department. My grandfather looked her in the eye and said, 'Baby, I'm going to build my empire. You should grab dinner with me.'"

"Oh, so that's where you get all your charm from?"

"Oh, I most certainly get it from my grandpa. He started his own construction company and made a name for himself in the greater Baltimore area. He sent my father to law school in Washington D.C., where he met my mom, and here I am."

"Look at that; it brought you here. I can't compete. I'm not even quite sure how my parents met. All I know is that they are in love, and I'm happy about that."

"That's all that matters then." I stared down at lower Manhattan's imperfect and jagged concrete. I was finished with my cigarette; in fact, I was over it a long time ago, but sometimes, you just have to suck it up.

"You're probably wondering why I smoke?" Azra asked.

"Why do you smoke?"

"I didn't always smoke, you know?"

"So, when did you start?"

"I started when I was fifteen. I guess the terrorist attacks on the World Trade Center didn't help. My father flew into New York just an hour before the attacks. Now, sometimes, if I'm outside and I hear a plane, it reminds me of my dad flying. I know, I sound silly."

"No, you don't sound silly at all."

"It's just… I needed a distraction. Sometimes I'll hear a car engine, and I just need something to take my mind off things. Of course, I chose the most addictive habit."

"Everyone's got something. I do that with soda."

"Soda?"

"Yeah, that's my distraction."

"Okay, well, let's walk back now. I hate soda, just letting you know."

The walk was short and quiet. We both wanted to get home. The awkward parts of the meeting were over, and it felt like we had known each other for a lifetime, whereas in reality, it had been only a few hours.

As we walked back inside the dorm, we were greeted by a security guard, half asleep with a fan blowing in his face so loud you would have thought the radiator needed repair maintenance. We made small talk in the elevator, nothing too heavy.

"This is us," Azra said. "C'mon, follow me."

Azra guided me into the room. The way her fingers stroked on my palms told me it was okay to be excited. Megan, her roommate, was walking out of the shower. Her hair was in a bun. She, too, was beautiful. Not as much as Azra, but a heartbreaker for the young men of New York City.

"Hey, I'm Megan,"

"Hi, Megan, I'm Max."

"Well, it's nice to meet you, Max. Already back at the dorm. That was quick, Azra, no?"

"Shut up, girlfriend, let me live," Azra said.

"Did you two eat?"

"Yes, Azra showed me her native food," I said. I felt as if that was my time to speak. I didn't want to sound like a robot, and I had to Megan some confidence.

"And was it good?"

"Very good," Azra said. She took the t-shirt she had worn to practice off. right in front of both of us. To say I was shocked would be an understatement. Her sports bra was a size to small—and, well, I was an eighteen-year-old athlete.

I took it upon myself to take a seat on the futon against the wall.

"This is a cool setup you two have here."

I couldn't help but play with the plastic that still outlined the legs of the futon. "We had one in our dorm as well, but my roommate, Kostas, brought his from home after years of wear and tear."

"Oh, is Kostas your roommate?" Megan asked excitedly.

"Yes, I'm sure you will meet him one day."

"Well, while Azra showers, would you like some dessert?"

"How can I say no?"

"Do you like brownies?"

"I love brownies!" I shot up from my seat. "Here, I can help you."

"No worries. I can take care of you. So, soccer player, huh? Which position do you play?

33

You look strong and athletic. Wait, are you a goalie?"

"Close," I said. "I play defense, but good guess."

"I'm not sure if Azra told you, but I was supposed to play on the team."

"She did tell me. I'm sorry it didn't work out."

"Oh no," Megan said. "I would never play a sport again."

"Oh yeah, I mean, trust me, you're not missing anything."

"Yeah. I'm a film major, and I've already met so many great friends."

"Oh, wow, film, that sounds exciting. What made you want to get into that?"

"I'm from Pittsburgh—go Steelers," Megan explained as she maneuvered around the kitchen. "I grew up watching all the Pittsburgh sports, and my brothers always told me that one day I could be in front of the camera." She paused, a faraway look in her eyes. "Hey, I'm going to cut you and Azra a brownie, is that okay?"

"Of course."

"Well, these are a little bit different."

"Well, it's college. I have to be open to try new things."

"Sounds like you have an amazing attitude."

"Well, not always," I said. "That's one of the things I'm working out as a college student."

Megan walked over a paper plate doubled up for extra support. "Let me know how it is."

Even though I had just eaten dinner, I was starving. Turkish cuisine was certainly not my thing, and although I enjoyed it, it was not nearly as filling as the kinds of food I was used to.

The shower water came to a halt as Megan sat down next to me with her plate. "Isn't college the best?"

A smile formed on my face. I flickered my eyes open and closed them even faster, like Christmas lights on a front lawn in late December. "This is the best brownie I've ever had."

Azra opened the door with her towel wrapped around her breasts. She looked mature beyond her years, smiling at us through the hallway like she knew something we didn't.

"Oh yeah, and do you smoke weed, too?" Megan asked.

"Smoke weed? I mean, no, well because of soccer and all."

"Oh well, you just ate that brownie," Megan reminded me. "I'm a tad bit confused."

"And?"

Azra put on a robe and made room next to the two of us. "It's a pot brownie, you moron."

"Like...marijuana?" I asked.

Azra mocked me as Megan laughed on. "Like marra-wanna?" they joked.

I started to giggle some more. "I'm not going to get in trouble for this, with the team, am I?"

"I like this boy," Megan said. "He's funny and cute."

"Relax, you're fine," Azra told me. "Max, I want to show you my view, it's insane."

I got up and continued to laugh. It was the first time I got high, and it was also the first time I was alone in a room with two women who thought I was cute.

As soon as I stepped into her room—considered big for Manhattan standards—I was met by floor to ceiling windows that overlooked Union Square. It was a million-dollar view that NYU leased for only 1,900 dollars a month.

"THE VIEW. THE VIEW," Azra screamed. "Isn't it just incredible?"

"I mean, it's beautiful." I had a similar room with a not-so-great view on a different building on a lower floor. But to an eighteen-year-old girl fascinated by the luxury of New York, it was her moment.

"Put your hands around me," Azra instructed.

I put my palms on her waist. Then, her hands guided my own further down her hips.

I looked up at her. "Is that good?"

Before she could answer, she demanded more from me. "Lay down," she yelled.

It was loud enough to get Megan moving towards the door. I could hear her footsteps on the hardwood floors as every pace led her one step closer to the door.

Knock, knock, knock.

"Azra, I'll shut the door."

"No, no, Megan, I'm going to need some help with this one. Please, if you will."

Megan came into the room, removing her sweatshirt in the process.

"My pleasure," Megan said as she approached me.

Azra kissed my neck as Megan began to unzip her pants in the background.

Could this really be happening? I thought to myself.

Azra took off her robe as she began to gently massage my ear lobe with her tongue.

"Just relax," she whispered.

Azra then turned around and grabbed Megan by the chin and kissed her as I stared on like a student on his first day of class.

"You're next," Megan said.

At that moment, Megan grabbed my biceps and forced them against the mattress. They both lifted my shirt over my arms and made love to me simultaneously. It was the greatest three and a half minutes of my life. At the time, that was all I knew, and it seemed normal to me that every college student may have or could have experienced that level of euphoria during the fall semester. I had nothing to compare it to, and quite frankly, I didn't want to compare it to anything.

That was the first time I had sex with Azra (and Megan), and it wouldn't be the last time the three of us made love together. This went on for the better half of our first year. I never told any of my teammates. Now, looking back, I suppose it would have given me some sort of "street cred," but as a teenager at NYU, that was the last thing anyone was looking for. The first romantic memory I had with Azra was shared with another person, which, unsurprisingly, ended up causing a lot of static between us.

Despite what most people would think about Azra and me, we were almost perfect together. She came to my games and cheered me on. As it turned out, she had made her ankle injury to be way worse than it was to score our date. She was back on the field just a week later. We were practically inseparable. We were kids, so young and so accessible, and brand new to the city. As exciting as this was, it was also intimidating and sometimes overbearing. But what we had was perfect for the inevitable stress of Manhattan. We relied on each other for late-night snacks and mid-day phone calls. Eventually, we trained together and challenged one another. Soccer was fun for the both of us—nothing less, nothing more. Most weeks, we made love twice a day, once before class and once after practice and before bed. Megan began to give us our space as she became preoccupied with traveling the city and meeting new men who sparked her romantic interest. Keep in mind, we were teenagers for a third of our college experience; it was effortless. We drank together and asked each other out to formals.

"SHE SAID YES!" I would yell outside the Starbucks.

"HE SAID YES!" she would say as we made our way to the deli next to our favorite theater.

We lived life to the fullest, and, most importantly, we stayed in the moment. We did not care too much for the past and never looked too far into the future. Azra would come home to my place in D.C. during the holidays because home was sometimes too far for her. I joined a fraternity my sophomore year, and she accepted a bid to a sorority shortly after. Being young and in love in New York City was electric, and soccer was just the icing on the cake.

The summers were rough. We spent about five to seven weeks apart, but when we came back for preseason in the fall, it was like we never left. The soccer story is how we met, but soccer also became a memory for both of us shortly after. Azra and I officially walked away from college soccer right before our junior seasons. This gave us more time to spend with one another, and when senior year came, we were ready to move in together. By the fall of our last year of undergrad, that was precisely what we did. We signed a lease together for a studio in the East Village.

Life was perfect, almost magical, and always exciting. We spent our mornings eating strawberries and reading the sports section of the newspaper. We went for afternoon strolls in the park, simply because we felt like it. We ate dinner on our fourth-floor balcony that hung over the strip of bars and comedy clubs. We stayed up late and talked about our dreams and what legacy we hoped to create for ourselves. We drank wine in bed, discussed our biggest fears, and debated our favorite films. We shared favorite albums and books. At that point, we had just turned twenty-one, but we were mature beyond our years. Sometimes, we would attend open houses with our Sunday best on towards the end of the weekend.

My parents loved her but hated the distance that separated our upbringings. It was true, I had everything a young man could hope for, but because I had never been to Turkey to meet her family, I was just a mystery man to her mother, father, and siblings. And for me, that was frightening. Still, things were going great—until one night in April, a month before we were set to graduate.

I can still recall the water on the nightstand half-finished. *I Love Lucy* was playing on repeat for the third time. We had Chinese food for dinner, and each of us had a bottle of Yuengling to wash it down. That night, we weren't as chatty as we usually were, but given the depths of our relationship, it wasn't suspicious—that is, until the morning hours.

Her phone rang at three a.m. Azra rolled out of bed and took the call. I was half asleep, thirsty, and my stomach was unsettled from the wonton soup I had slurped down just hours before. My eyes flickered open and closed like an old, rustic, and scratchy black and white film. I could hear her showering shortly after she woke up. As my mind wandered, I was brought back to the first time we hung out in her dorm room as freshmen. The handle twisting and turning. The water flowed rapidly without warning. The twelve-dollar shower curtain was dragged into the moisture only to fall back into its original place slowly. Azra's shower took only forty-five seconds if that. As she stepped out, another call came in. She took that, too.

"Okay, okay, calm down. I understand. I will get everything ready now," Azra said. Her pitch was loud enough to fully wake me from any dream or nightmare I may have been experiencing.

I finally got up, even though I didn't want to. "What's going on?"

"You're going to think this is crazy, but my mom bought me an international flight for 11:00 a.m. I have a few hours to pack everything I need. I have to go home."

"Wait, okay, slow down, Azra."

"I can't go into detail, but it's family-related. It's serious."

"Well, if it's serious, I want to be there for you."

"I can't tell you everything right now," Azra said as she unzipped a suitcase she'd taken down from the overhead closet. It still had tags on it from the last time she traveled.

"I mean, you have to. Azra, you have to," I said as I chased her around our narrow yet spacious studio. Her sighs grew heavier, and her steps became less limited.

"I love you very much, okay. I do love you," Azra said, almost in tears.

"Azra, you're acting insane. What is going on?"

"No, no, Max, you don't get to accuse me of insanity, not right now," Azra said as she stopped packing for three seconds and stared me directly in the eye. "I told you, it's family. My family comes first."

"And I'm not family?" I asked.

"Max, I met you freshman year. I haven't even known you for four full years. You've never even met my parents in person."

"And whose fault is that?" I asked. "I have wanted to visit for years now."

"It's not that simple."

"Then, maybe I'm missing something?"

"Maybe you are!" she screamed back.

"Let's just take a deep breath, both of us just got a little excited there. Let's slow it down. I think we both just have been really busy and haven't had time to communicate."

"Well, I always communicate."

"Oh, what? And I don't?"

"I don't have time for this. I have a lot to take care of." Azra looked around, making sure she didn't leave anything of significance behind. Her focus was on the task at hand, not on our future. This became more and more clear with every bag she packed, with every step she took.

"What about graduation?"

"I have enough credits. I'm not worried about that. Don't worry, I'll be back. I promise."

"This whole thing isn't adding up. Look at me!"

"Max, what?"

Azra looked into my eyes, but only because I demanded she do so. There was something she was hiding from me. In that moment, even though neither of us spoke, a dialogue was exchanged through our eyes.

"You're just going to go to Istanbul, and you're telling me I don't have a right to know why?"

"Family is different, Max. It's something that you're going to have to respect."

Azra had used the *family* card a few times too many. And regardless of the severity of why she was going, or despite what I believed, I murmured words of loyalty under my breath. *"I trust you."*

"And I trust you, too," Azra said. "I'll Skype you right when I get to Turkey"

Azra called a cab at around 8 a.m. to take her to JFK International Airport. I tried falling back to sleep but my anxiety kept me up. I wanted to believe that Azra leaving was just a bad nightmare that I temporarily had to live through. When I looked over at the nightstand, I saw Azra's lipstick tattooed on the glass of water. The moisture began to drip down and fall to the rustic wood on the corner of the Ikea carpentry. I had to finally wake up and face the music. I wasn't going to see Azra for a very long time.

Chapter 3: The Aftershock
April 2015

I paced around my balcony, above the hustle and flow of a laid-back East Village, giving me a chance to think while not feeling totally alone. I was overwhelmed with paranoia and self-doubt. I thought perhaps she left because of something I had done in the past, potentially something she found out about, something I was unaware had happened.

"Could it be?" I said out loud. "No, no that's not it."

I picked up a Washington Nationals Inaugural Opening Day replica baseball bat and let it rest gently on my shoulders. I choked up all the way on the grip like I was stepping into the home run derby in mid-July. I grabbed my fitted Yankees cap from my closet and put it on tight and let the interlocking *NY* shine directly over my forehead. Although I was raised in the DMV area, New York had a way of stealing your mind. This represented the dualistic approach to who Azra and I were. Our lives were separated by where we met and where we came from

"Was it something I did?" I asked out loud. "Maybe it's something I didn't do?"

I choked up a little further on the bat. Our light that lit up the entire living room and bed stood in my peripheral vision. It just looked so appealing and tasty. I brought back my bat and did my best Alex Rodriguez impersonation. The bulb stood no chance, but the feeling of regret immediately overcame my body.

"Fuck," I screamed.

I dragged my hands through my hair. I had above-average locks at this stage in my life, but they had been annoying me for the longest time, and this was the perfect excuse to start over. I ripped off my shirt, dropped to the floor, and did thirty pushups. I considered myself to be in good shape, but that was the first time I dropped for a bodyweight workout since had I left the soccer team. I knocked the thirty out as quickly as possible and dragged my body to the bathroom. I yelled out another expletive. I felt the anger that had been bottled up inside of me for years. Anger and frustration can sometimes appear synonymous, but this was anger in its purest form. I placed my palms on the bathroom sink and slowly lifted my face towards the mirror. I was brought back to all the trials and tribulations that our relationship faced. It had only been an hour, but I was already feeling the weeks and months of stress that would naturally follow. I ran my palms through my hair one last time and lifted the glass door that acted as a medicine cabinet. I took out the electric razor and ran it through the middle of my scalp. The hair fell to the floor. I faded the sides out as best as I could, impressed by my precision. I cranked the hot water just a tad bit further to the left. I ran the water through my new hair style but realized there was not much to lift off, although my hair did have a nice glisten to it in the light. I quickly turned off the water in the sink and made my way to the shower. I ripped my shorts off and waited for the water to heat up as I craved the cleansing—physically and spiritually. I could still smell Azra's fragrance in the room. The shampoo that I never let her try on me was now something I couldn't wait to use on my new scalp. The conditioner bottle that was the size of a toothpaste container was now a friendly reminder of everything she left behind, all wrapped up in a familiar scent. Yet, still, I was happy to wash off and come up with a plan.

I quickly got out and wrapped the towel tightly around my waist, my body still strong but crippled by the thought of losing my first love. I walked to the kitchen and grabbed an easy mac out of the pantry. I opened it up and threw it in the microwave. I didn't feel like getting dressed, at least for now. I opened my MacBook, and immediately, music started blasting through YouTube. It was a playlist Azra had started before she left. The songs were pleasant, but the messages of the stories pissed me off. I slammed the screen down. But at the bottom, I saw the red light come on. The warm flash was a friendly reminder to plug the device in before it crashed. I skipped towards the closet and grabbed my high school basketball shorts. I slipped on my sandals and grabbed the charger, but my left slide wasn't on tight. I fell and hit my knee on the corner of the fireplace. I was hurt but not injured. I must have said the F word over twenty times. I laid down and accepted defeat. I looked up to the ceiling fan, the cool air was a reminder that the spring was starting to heat up.

"Why me, God, why me? Why did you take her from me?"

I could have laid down for hours and wallowed in self-pity. It would have been easy, the acceptable way to handle a breakup in our society. But instead, I thought back to my competitive soccer days as a defenseman. Those moments when you had almost no gas left in the tank, but you were still on full blast. That's when I realized I had to do something. I had to act fast. The computer was heating back up, which meant some juice was loading back into the device. Immediately, a light bulb went on—both in my head and on the home screen.

"Twitter!" I yelled out to myself.

Azra's username was already signed in. It was too good to be true, yet still worth the investigation.

"C'mon, c'mon, c'mon," I yelled.

Twitter logged me right in. I went into her recent messages. Azra was five steps ahead of me and it showed. There were only three threads open; I was one of them, and Megan was next, below me.

"What the hell?" I asked out loud when my eyes stopped on the third message thread.

"Who is Yusef?"

I was only met with silence. After all, when you live alone, there is no one to answer your calls or solve your problems.

I scrolled into his profile: @_dOnttAskk_Y_5

I was now dragged into another world. Yusef.

Before I read the messages, I decided it would be best to have some context about what I was about to get myself into. Luckily, for me, Yusef (or Yu) had a Facebook page. Most of the photos were of Yusef and his friends on the swim team. Others were at the pro basketball arenas in what appeared to be in Istanbul. Yusef appeared to be athletic and lengthy, no taller than six foot five but certainly no shorter than six one. He had a dark complexion with thick hair. He didn't look like the men here in New York. He had a cut physique up close, but if I was asked to describe him from fifty feet away, I would say he was skinny and angular. He wore a hat in some of his older photos, but you could tell he recently outgrew that phase—his hair was well maintained, probably by a local barbershop or a salon somewhere downtown. Eventually, I made it to the last few profile pictures. They were blurry but they were still clear enough to make out who was in them. I came to the last photo, and there she was. It was Azra.

Still, I couldn't bring myself to view the Twitter messages…yet.

Chapter 4: A Global Pandemic

March 2020

Over the years, I tried desperately to erase Azra from my mind. I dated new girls, I traveled around the country to visit high school friends I had previously lost touch with. But still, nothing seemed to fix the void that Azra had left in my heart, not to mention the gap she left in my self-purpose. For almost four years, all through college, I shared every moment with Azra—the highs, the lows, and everything in between. I had to confront who I was, maybe for the first time ever, as an adult in New York City.

So, instead of biting the bullet, I cracked a Bud Light and swallowed it quickly as I prepared myself for inevitable defeat. I opened up Twitter, and there it was—Azra. She was still logged in. What I did not expect was for their conversations to have been taking place all throughout our relationship.

[October 2012]
"Hey, Azra."
"Hey, Yusef, how have you been?"
"Great, and how have you been, Azra?"
"Great, can we talk tomorrow? About to sleep."
"Sure. Goodnight."

I cracked another beer, and this time, I made it an obligation to consume half of it right away.

"Here we go," I said to myself as I scrolled down to finish the rest of the thread.

[January 2013]
"Happy New Year, Azra!"
"Happy New Year, Yusef!"
"How have you been?"
"Good, busy with school, you?"
"Busy with swim team," Yusef added.
"How is that going?"
"It's going lol."
"(Smiley face emoji)," Azra wrote.
"How is nursing school going?"

That is when I had to stop to finish my beer. It wasn't the conversation in it of itself but rather the subject in which they were speaking. How Azra was living this romantic, and what I thought to be, wonderful life here in New York, but at the same time, she was speaking so enthusiastically to a lover from home. It was all eerie and suspicious.

[February 2013]
"It's going great. But I miss home. I miss you," Azra said.
"I miss you, too, Azi," Yusef replied.

"Azi?" I asked out loud. "Never heard Azi before, that's a new one."

I reached into the fridge and dug out the box of Coors Light bottles that I had purchased on sale from the bodega down the block. I sat all six bottles on the table and wasn't too concerned with the temperature. Jealousy has a funny way of forcing a man to drink quicker than usual.

"Let's talk soon, okay?" Azra followed.

Their conversation was melodic and soothing to read, even from someone who should hate this man. Yet, still, I clicked my phone and opened it up to my home screen. A photo of Azra and me in Madison Square Park sitting under an umbrella with Starbucks coffees in our hands were in the background of my apps and messaging platforms. I wondered if she had the same background. In some ways, the thought of her virtually removing me from her life scared me more than her not being here.

I cracked open another drink, and this time, it went down smooth, almost like water. I realized I was entering a zone that would be hard to come back from. I needed a distraction, and because this was my first time living alone, I used the television to escape, a way to "catch my breath" for a minute. I turned on MSNBC and was immediately reeled into the coverage of Covid-19—a deadly virus strain that was disrupting life as we knew it, not just in New York City but throughout the globe. That's when the field correspondent reported on a possible shutdown of international flights in the next few weeks. I knew that I had to keep scrolling, even if the truth hurt. I scrolled and scrolled. My curiosity thickened to some of the small talk, yet instead, I made my way over to the spring of 2015, right before our graduation was set to take place.

> [April 2015]
> "Hey, Azra??"
> "Yes?"
> "Something happened, can you talk?"
> "Yes, call me now if you have to."
> "Dialing you as we speak."

Truthfully speaking, I was on the edge of my seat. In some ways, the stories our loved ones keep from us open a curiosity we may have never experienced had we never met that person. And so, I scrolled further to read the rest, but that was it, that was the end of the thread. Or maybe, just quite possibly, this was my first clue. But how many clues were there? That was the major question I had struggled with. Was Azra so intelligent that she left her Twitter login open, knowing that I would have a quarter-life crisis and search
for the answers all these years later? She always was a bright girl, but this bright? I don't believe that anyone throughout history is this smooth and certainly not this strategic. And then, suddenly,

something clicked. Right below the thread between Azra and what had appeared to be her longtime ex-boyfriend was the conversation between Azra and her first roommate, Megan. I polished off another Coors Light. The buzz was already settled; at this point, I was just drinking to keep myself company.

[February 2020]

"Wait I minute," I said. "This is recent, isn't it?"

I knocked over the remaining beer that was left in the bottle and lifted my laptop before the liquid took care of the rest. My computer was on its last year or two, but I made it this long, might as well see it through. I grabbed an old Sports Illustrated and damped it on the man-made puddle that now formed between the coasters and the deck of cards.

"Jesus," I yelled. "This is ridiculous."

I got up and made my way towards the pantry in search of a fresh roll of paper towels. I remembered an extra roll in the bathroom under the sink where I kept an emergency stash, Febreze, and random shower travel accessories. Some items had overextended their stay, not because they lacked utility, but because of some of the nostalgia they carried. One of these was a travel soap case. Azra had gotten it for me before our first trip together as a couple. Maybe it was a symbolic purchase for the journeys that lay ahead, or maybe it was just a soap case. Yet, with those two questions spinning around my head, I dared to ask more. What if it was a clue? So, before I could pick up the paper towel, I tucked the soap case under my armpit as I made my way back towards the coffee table. I sat back down, took a deep breath, and collected my thoughts. I shook the container but noticed a void within the gap. I ripped it open and two shiny pieces of paper fell to the floor as the air sent them under the couch. Immediately, I dropped to the floor as my knees cracked. I was able to go into the pushup formation and use my arm to grab the loose pieces. I focused as I tried to make the Polaroid out.

"Megan?" I said out loud.

Sometimes I forgot how big of a deal Megan was to Azra. She was her first roommate, her first real friend in the states. As college concludes and the pressure of the real world settles in, we lose our school friends, and Azra and Megan were the perfect example of just that. In fact, Azra left Megan, to be brutally honest, yet there was always a tremendous loyalty shown to Azra from Megan even after just one year of sharing living arrangements.

The photo of Azra and Megan could not have been a day past November 2011, as it was marked "Halloween frosh year," in red Sharpie on the white strip that gave the perfect header and footer for what today would be an Instagram caption. I remember that Halloween like it was yesterday; soccer was concluding, and the festivities were a big deal as a newbie in Manhattan, specifically as NYU underclassmen. For undergrad students and mainly undeclared scholars, Halloween was the New Year's Eve ball drop to a tourist. The day was spent discussing potential plans and meeting for drinks as the night was reserved for promiscuous fun and apartment loft showings that some of the foreign students from royalty threw despite their separated parents. Ultimately, Halloween was an unofficial mid semester break, an excuse to let one's guard down in hopes of finding the perfect rooftop as the fall air made you feel alive before winter's inevitable harnessing of concrete. So, with nostalgia and memories creeping in, I took another gulp, and another one, and one more. I then felt a thick sticky substance on the back of the photograph. It was a photo of me and some of my buddies from the NYU soccer team on the same Halloween with the titled caption *1998* on the Polaroid.

"1998?" I said out loud. I took another sip of my Coors Light. I had one left on the coffee table, so I had to make it last.

"What was I dressed as? A velociraptor?"

I analyzed the photo, this time more thoroughly than the last.

"Godzilla?" I questioned as I took a deep chug. The film was released in 1998, so the date was starting to make sense. The toxins from the drink hit me so quickly that I clenched my forehead. "Godzilla?" I thought. "That's it, Godzilla."

Godzilla was the first movie Azra and I watched together, and it became symbolic as time went on. Godzilla was a New York movie, and I think that's why we left it on and finished it through. It was more about poking fun at the acting and laughing at some of the unrealistic action shots that made us relish the film. Even though the movie was fifteen years old at the time, it was a first viewing for the two of us. It made our worlds slow down every time we put it on, or at least that's what Azra used to say. There was always that one scene in particular that Azra pointed out, the site next to the Flatiron building where shots were ordered by the sergeant to be fired at Godzilla. However, many of the bullets missed the monster and hit the Flatiron Building so many times that it caused the famous New York City landmark to explode. Anyways, Azra loved the Flatiron Building; she was fascinated by not only its history but by its physical presence. The way it stood in view of the park and how it divided the two paths of direction that you could take in the city. It was defined and the only building in New York City that was named for what it really looked like in real life, and that is, an *iron*. Azra always used to say, "It's where the city splits." And she was right. When you looked on the map and saw the Flatiron Building, it was an option you had in life—left or right? It didn't matter which direction you went, because, at that point, you had to choose something.

I couldn't sit around in my apartment any longer. I grabbed my black fleece that was kept on the kitchen counter for times like this. I checked to see if my keys were secure in my back hip, I knew they were there, but there was something about double-tapping each compartment that made me comfortable before exiting my apartment.

The dusk scene in the Financial District was something out of a movie. Restaurants prepared outdoor seating in the spring, a reminder of the fun times to come. And yet, there was a certain aura in the air that I had yet to experience in NYC. My phone vibrated in my pocket—an alert from Yahoo Finance.

"The coronavirus may enter the United States quicker than experts expected," the colorful Yahoo app alerted me.

"Where to, sir?"

"Flatiron," I said.

"That's a big area, my friend. You have an address?"

"Oh sorry." I adjusted my jacket and took out my wallet to make sure I had my ID and cash sorted out. "Yes. The Flatiron Building."

I put my hand through the transparent plastic slide that separated the driver from the passenger. I handed the man two twenty-dollar bills. I figured the ride would only amount to twenty-seven or thirty dollars max, but when you're unemployed, you ironically lose concept of money and begin to exchange unwarranted tips.

"Thank you, my friend. Thank you, thank you."

The ride was quiet for the first few minutes. I did not mind; the silence was normal to me and, in some ways, calming. But then, as those initial thoughts of stillness settled in, I looked up towards the driver's armrest and saw a few interesting items scattered across the passenger seat. There were pens, pencils, notepads, and a flag stuck between the awkward gap where iPhones and AirPods fell through. I called it "no man's land." I had seen the flag before but couldn't remember exactly where I had seen it. It was a simplistic yet bold banner. It featured a white star and a crescent. Immediately, I remembered where I first saw the emblem. It was hung against the wall of the freshman bathroom at the NYU dorms. I can still remember Megan ripping it down after she had too many drinks on St. Patty's Day during the spring semester of our freshman year, back in 2012. I had to Google it quickly to make sure I wasn't imagining things. "The Flag of Turkey colors," I spelled out.

Did you mean The Flag of Turkey? Google spat back at me with the correct spelling, forming the appropriate response to my inquiry. But, even so, I didn't have to correct Google—the images were proof of my memory from close to a decade back. It was true, it was the flag of Turkey. With my suspicion confirmed, I thought about remaining quiet, but after all, there was traffic on the side streets and the temptation of killing a few minutes was almost irresistible.

"Are you from there?" I asked.

"From where?" the driver responded.

"Turkey?" I asked, this time with a more specific location.

"Oh yes, yes, have you ever been?"

"Oh no, I just used to know someone from there, that's all."

"Oh, girlfriend, former lover?"

"How'd you know?"

"Well, I see boy from America, how could one resist an exotic woman from Turkey?"

"I think you nailed it. That was the initial appeal."

"Ah, and then? You two, fall in love?"

"Yeah, we were together for a while."

Then there was a pause for about fifteen seconds, just long enough to lose my train of thought.

"Name?" the driver asked.

"Max," I responded.

The driver looked confused. "The girlfriend?"

"Oh, Azra," I told the driver.

"Azra, yes, beautiful name. My grandmother's name is Azra, a popular name in Turkey. Where is she now?"

"Azra?"

"Yes, your former girlfriend, Azra?"

"I really have no idea. Her old roommate was nice, she's here somewhere in New York, I think."

"Her old roommate you say, does she like you?"

"Megan? Oh no, I mean, maybe as a friend, perhaps."

"I see, I see, so ultimately you're chasing Azra, it sounds?"

"Chasing Azra?" I said out loud. "Well, when you put it like that, I guess you have a point."

"Nothing wrong with chasing someone. Many wise men will tell you to hide, do the opposite of chase, but you, you're too young to stay put," the driver wisely advised.

"So, you think it's smart?"

"I never said smart."

There was an awkward silence, a gap in dialogue between the driver and me.

"So, you dated this Azra girl, you ever visit Turkey?"

"No, I have never been."

"How long did you two date?"

"Around four years."

"That's too bad, Turkey is very beautiful.

Well, you work? Maybe now is the time to go before the coronavirus makes its way."

"I don't think the coronavirus is going to affect anything here."

"Oh, you are sadly mistaken, my friend. This virus is going to be bad."

"Well, even so, not sure what's in it for me to go to Turkey."

"Do you love her?"

"Azra?"

"Yes," the driver looked back in hopes of an answer.

"I do, and I've been missing her a lot lately. I've been getting signs… I don't know why I'm telling you all of this…but thank you for listening."

"No worries. Is this good, Flatiron building up ahead?"

"This is perfect, thanks again."

"It's okay to chase," the driver said as he sped off.

"That was so incredibly strange," I said out loud. I walked towards the iron-shaped building and enjoyed the solace and comfort of having the freedom, having the time to myself.

The Flatiron Building stood boldly in between two edges of the city. It truly was a beautiful structure—outdated, yes, but its surroundings were modern and contemporary. Everything about this area of the city reminded me of Azra, and it wasn't just because of the time we spent together in Madison Square Park, but instead, the flow. Beautiful women walked by in their high heels as restaurants served meals and catered to the city's elite. The Flatiron encompassed NYC grit and glamour, and the two combined together were a lethal combo. If anything, I resembled both the grit and (wannabe) glamour that the Big Apple offered. It reminded me of a famous show that Azra and I watched often, Sex and The City, where Carrie says, *"In New York, they say, you're always looking for a job, a relationship or an apartment. So, let's say you have two out of the three and they're fabulous. Why do we let the thing we don't have affect how we feel about all the things we do have? Why does one minus a plus one feel like it adds up to zero?"*

In college, not having a job left us with two out of the three, not bad, at least in theory. But now, I felt as if the thirty-three percent I was lacking was a pretty depressing number to pride myself on. Yet, even so, this time, I was looking for food or a quick bite to keep me at ease. There were many restaurants in the area but something about grabbing fast food with a generous severance package, felt, well, beneath me. I wanted to sit down, listen to a podcast, and catch my breath. That's when I saw a formal yet delicious restaurant getting ready for the dinner rush but cleaning up from the lunch gatherings.

"Amazing" I said out loud. "This is what I need." As I approached a pretty and quaint restaurant.

The door made a CLINK, as I approached the hostess podium. I smiled and looked around as all the waitresses glanced over in my direction. I scrolled through my phone to pass the time. It wasn't long before a beautiful, most likely college freshman or sophomore, greeted me with a menu.

"Hello, sir!" the hostess shouted. "Welcome to Obica, how can I be of assistance today?"

"Hi, yes," I said as I collected my thoughts. "I'm sorry, I thought I recognized someone from the distance."

"That's okay, so how can I help you?"

"Could I do a table in the back by myself?"

"Sure, we are relatively quiet right now, so just follow me."

The petite, blonde hostess had an engaging aura to her. She was extremely professional yet polite—an attractive and pleasant combination.

"This is perfect. Oh, do you have a WiFi password that I could grab, if it's not too much trouble, of course?"

"Sure, it's right on the back of the menu."

"You're the best," I said. The words sounded corny, but I was hungry and frustrated, and working behind a desktop computer in finance for the past handful of years made me immune to awkward and cliché conversations.

"Just doing my job. I'm guessing you're going to need a few minutes to look over the menu?"

"Well, for now, could I grab a Peroni, oh, and maybe a glass of Coke on the side?"

"Sure, we actually don't have Peroni, but we have Coke."

"Stella then?"

"We do have Stella."

"Works for me."

"I'll be back in a few."

Killing time when you go out to eat by yourself never makes any sense nor is it an easy task. There's something so inorganic about scrolling through ESPN scores and social media that can make a man sweat through his t-shirt. But then, what happened next made me realize that fate and opportunity, although rarely coinciding, were happening at this restaurant. It was Megan. Her hair swayed in the background while her black thick work shoes elevated her height a few inches. From a distance, she appeared tall.

"Megan?" I said.

"Max? What are you doing here?"

"I kind of want to ask you the same thing?"

"I've been working here for the last five years now. Just on the side. Wait, so how are you? What's it been?"

"Probably five years, now that I think about it."

"Five years since I've last seen you?"

"I guess college graduation, in 2015, after—"

"After Azra left?"

"Yeah, after Azra left. Have you spoken to Azra?"

"No, she is as much of a ghost to me as she is to you."

"How come?"

"What do you mean?"

"How come you haven chased after her?"

"What do you think I'm doing now?"

"So, you, at the restaurant I work at, is chasing Azra?"

"Yeah, I got some clues from her. Nothing crazy, but big enough to make me think and re-open the envelope."

"So, what's your envelope looking like now?"

"Well, I saw something. It was about Godzilla. I know, it's silly."

"No, tell me, now I'm curious."

"Well, if you must know, Godzilla was the first film Azra and I watched together as a couple."

"And?"

"There's this scene where the Flatiron Building explodes...and it's a real long story, so I came down here and got hungry, and now I'm surprised to see you."

"Why are you surprised to see me?"

"Not surprised, just—"

"Okay, well, not every graduate from NYU goes on to make a boatload of money after college."

"I actually was just laid off from my job due to Covid-19, and my apartment in the Financial District isn't exactly cheap."

"Well, that sucks."

"Yeah, don't remind me."

"Wait, don't you work in finance? How were you affected?"

"Honestly, I couldn't tell you. I think my boss was just looking to cut back. He's not the smartest managing director. They're not all smart, believe it or not."

"This Covid-19 thing…"

"Yeah, it's pretty scary. What are your thoughts on it?"

"I think it's going to be really bad. Three weeks from now I think this restaurant will close down and I'll be without a job again for the fifth time in five years."

"That bad, huh?"

"It's not good."

"Should I start wearing a mask?"

"Yeah, I actually have an extra in my bag. But I'll let you eat in peace."

"Wait, Megan, hold on."

"Yeah?"

"Be honest. What do you think I should do, you know, with Azra?"

"You want the honest truth?"

"I want your raw advice."

"Well, before everything shuts down, go to Istanbul. You're looking for clues here, and that's great and all, but you won't find Azra in New York."

"So, you're telling me that before the world shuts down, I should hop on a plane and fly to Turkey?"

"That is exactly what I'm telling you. But I know you won't go, so it's easy for me to say. I mean, I wouldn't actually go; it's just that in theory, it sounds like a great adventure."

"But I've never been there, not even when we dated."

"That's exactly, well, in theory, why you need to go there now."

"You really think I should spontaneously hop on a plane to Eastern Europe during all of this madness?"

"I guess it depends on how badly you want to find her, or how willing you are to chase her around."

"Well, it doesn't sound as great when you say it like that."

The waitress came back with my drink. "Sorry, am I interrupting something here?"

"Oh, we were just catching up, sweetheart," Megan added. "Here, take my number. Do you remember Azra's cousin who came to visit when we were freshmen?"

"Oh yeah, Demir or something?"

"Yes, Demir. Well, Demir has a restaurant in Istanbul, and it's brand new—I still follow his page. He always thought you were a nice boy for Azra, and I'm sure he would love to see you."

"I'll consider it."

Megan then handed me a ripped piece of green paper that was used for writing checks. On it was her number with a smiley face written out with two dots and an umbrella figurine. "In case you don't have my updated contact."

"Thanks."

"Well, I have to head back to work. Oh, enjoy whatever it is your ordering. Let's keep in touch."

My waitress came back to check on me as soon as Megan walked away.

"Everything okay here?"

"Oh, everything is perfect," I said. "Actually, just a quick question."

"Yeah, of course?"

"I was just wondering, is Megan seeing anybody?"

The young waitress threw me a look of discomfort and disdain. "I'm sorry but who wants to know?"

"Oh, it's not even like that. I used to date Megan's best friend. I'm just curious."

"I'm new here, but Megan is definitely single, I can tell you that much."

"Okay, thank you."

The young waitress went on her way, most likely rolling her eyes at having to deal with annoying customers like myself.

Chapter 5: Safe Travels

March 2020

Unemployment was a hazy blur. My isolation became my only friend. Living alone had its perks, but it did become lonely. The elevator was the worst. It was a friendly reminder of just how abandoned I was. Couples would kiss as the lights on the side lit up. You could smell the cologne and perfume fuse together—the perfect mix of New York City. If Brooklyn and Manhattan had a kid, it would be the above-average couple who lived just a floor below me.

"Thank God," I yelled out as I dangled my keys. "I love you, no, I love you," I mocked.

As I lifted my key into the top slot (I never locked the bottom), I salivated over the bourbon that sat on my bar cart with the view of the Freedom Tower in the distance. Who needed a significant other when you have New York City, right?

"Hey, Alexa, play, I don't know, play..."

"I'm sorry, I tried looking for 'I don't know play' and no matches were found."

"Alexa, play Frank Sinatra, New York, New York."

I looked out to the skyline of downtown and let out a sigh of relief before I poured the bourbon into the rocks of ice that dominated the top half of my glass set that Azra had purchased for our apartment in the East Village just years prior.

"God that's good," I said as the alcohol caressed my lips, and my head shook from the aftertaste. "That's it."

I immediately opened my laptop and sat there aimlessly, not knowing what was next. I stared at the screen and was mesmerized by the alert on my work Gmail account: "Sorry, we cannot access the proper field to this account." My competitive side kicked in.

"Fuck this," I yelled.

I swung the drink down my throat and cracked open a bag of Doritos, pouring it into a party bowl with reckless abandon as the spare players fell onto my kitchen floor.

I scrolled onto Instagram and saw old teammates and friends from college who were moving on with their lives. "*Officially signed our first lease together*" or "*Two years together and I can't wait for many more.*"

But, for me, life was repetitive and mundane. However, I would be lying if I said it came without excitement and the occasional dose of adrenaline. As much as I was emotional about Azra, I had never been this much in tune with seeking answers from the past. And so, with every sip, I was brought back to my former self. Time and possessions collided, just as they were always meant to intervene.

I closed my laptop screen, unbuttoned my pants, and let air in. But, for some reason, in that moment, I let frustration overcome me.

"FUCKKKKKKKKKKKK!" I yelled. "FUCK YOU, AZRA."

I stepped out to my balcony that overlooked lower Manhattan. Traffic and sirens rang loudly despite my frustrations.

"AZRA, ah!" I screamed at the top of my lungs. The rich college girl from four or five units away looked on in dismay. I shook my glass in her face, smiled, and kept my eyes open as I downed the drink, watching her stare back at me.

"Yeah, yeah, you will grow up one day," I whispered.

I let my elbows rest on the balcony and envisioned what it would be like if Azra was with me now in this very exact moment. I wondered if she would be proud, if she would brag to her friends that I was, in fact, her boyfriend. I also wondered if maybe she'd be embarrassed about my most recent layoff but impressed by my cozy severance package. I thought about what she would think about my MBA degree from Columbia, if she would think I was just wasting my time. I can picture her saying, "Why not law school like your father?" But that scenario was merely a fantasy at this point.

I turned the TV on from outside. I had no dog, so my television served as my only form of companion, whether it be Tucker Carlson or Anderson Cooper.

"Today, March 24, 2020, the stock market has tumbled..." the Fox News anchor reported.

That headline caught my attention. As someone who worked in the markets, I knew that this virus was officially the real deal. I poured another glass and sat down in front of my laptop.

Flight to Istanbul

Instantly, five to ten flight options appeared.

Tickets start as low as $349.99.

So, I went deeper into the flight details.

"Okay, Newark to Istanbul, tomorrow at three p.m."

I clicked the flight's availability.

Are you sure you want to proceed?

"Yes"

I click *agree.*

Hello, please enter in the details of your credit card information.

I entered my information.

Sorry, our system could not match your credentials.

It was my security code.

"C'mon, c'mon, c'mon."

Congratulations, your flight is confirmed for tomorrow at 6:15 A.M. EST—(9H 20 + minutes) – Istanbul Airport.

Thank you, you will receive a confirmation email immediately. If you do not receive an email in your inbox in 5 minutes, please check your spam folder.

I shut my laptop and opened my iPhone, checking my email immediately.

"Let's go," I yelled out. "I'm going to Turkey!" I ran back onto my balcony "Holy shit, I'm actually going to Istanbul. I have to pack."

I ran into my room and busted my closet door wide open. I pushed through old tax forms and boxes that held high school accolades and awards. I shoved some old dress clothes to the side and made my way to my Samsonite carry-on. It was small enough to travel in comfort but bulky enough to carry the basics.

"Oh, what a beautiful sight it is."

Then, suddenly, my phone lit up. "Hey, it's Megan, turns out I had your number."

I flipped my phone over on its back so I wouldn't have to confront the inevitable. I ran back and poured myself another drink.

"Screw it," I said as I threw another round back.

"Well, what are you waiting for?" I texted Megan with a wink face after the question mark.

Megan replied with two wink emojis, and I proceeded to send her my address. So, just like any other selfish young man, I started packing in hopes of beating her anticipated arrival. I stacked up my fresh round of laundry and stuffed it into the bag. I rolled up five pairs of socks and a couple of dress shirts and one pair of crisp dress shoes that I wore to my NYU graduation. I held my passport in my hand and contemplated where I should keep it in the meantime.

"I'm outside, I'm here," Megan texted.

I brushed my teeth quickly and left my passport inside the shelf of my bathroom mirror.

"Coming," I responded.

I lifted my pants, adjusted my posture, and got ready to take the elevator down, just as Megan appeared outside my door.

"Oh, you're here-here?" I said.

"I just told your doormen that I was here for you, and they sent me right up. Is that a problem?"

"No, no problem at all."

"Wow, nice place," Megan said. She walked around like she was in her favorite museum.

"Here, let me get you a glass of wine. White or red?"

"C'mon, Max, it's me, I haven't changed that much."

"Red it is then."

Megan loved bold colors. When I met her as a freshman, she usually stuck with dark purple clothes, the same colors of NYU. But, as we got deeper into our college years, she moved to mostly black and darker shades of grey.

"So, this is your place?"

"Yeah, is that a good *so* or a bad *so*?"

"Good, really good. I mean how do you afford all of this?"

"Um, hello, NYU? Does that ring any bells?"

"Yeah, I should have studied business."

Megan took a sip of her wine and looked out the window. She started to wave her hands towards her eyes as if she needed air.

"Are you okay, Megan?"

"Yeah, yeah, I'm fine," she said as she began to cry. "It's just that, you have all this and dress nice, and I'm sure all the girls want to be with you, and I'm in my late twenties, serving food. I live in a pre-war walkup, and I haven't been laid in two months."

It was certainly a lot to take in, and I had a sensitive side, but not with someone like Megan. Even though I wasn't totally surprised by what Megan was telling me.

"Oh, come on. Two months? A girl as pretty as you? I don't buy it. Besides, some people choose to pay more for a walk up...they say it has more charm, or so I've heard."

Megan laughed and wiped her tears. "Look at you, Max, you still kept your charm and humor. You never let anything bring you down. That's why you have all of this."

Megan grabbed my chin and massaged the whiskers that rested above my throat, just north of my chin. Finally, she brought my eyes down towards hers and kissed me. Our lips and tongues embraced for seven or eight seconds until I pushed her away.

"I'm sorry," I said. "It's just that..."

"No, it's my fault, I'm so stupid." Megan took off her jacket that covered her toned shoulders. Megan was no stranger to a fitness center or yoga glass. She threw her glass of wine back and looked back at me. "Fuck it," she yelled as she kissed my neck.

As much as times had changed, some things remained the same, and I could still remember the first night I was with Azra, with Megan joining in. I always kept that moment to myself, but now things were coming full circle. Megan took my clothes off and kept half of hers on. There was something so relaxing about how she made love, as if she got pleasure from seeing me at ease.

Megan was an artist at heart, and the way she expressed herself physically was the same way a painter bled out on a canvas.

"Can I be extra loud?" she asked.

"No one can hear us," I whispered back.

Megan had a way of taking control without being too aggressive. Her balance was exactly right, like a musician on a subway car playing their tunes, slow and steady.

We both only lasted about seven minutes, but it felt like we made love for an eternity. Every second was filled with passion from moments of our past, the pleasure rooted mostly in nostalgia.

"How was it?" Megan said with a smirk as she pulled my blankets up over her breasts.

Her chest was beautiful, and her body had become even more appealing as she got older; but unlike most guys, that's not what attracted me to Megan. I think it was her mindset and carefree lifestyle that I so genuinely craved.

"It was incredible, Megan, it really was."

"Wow, that's high praise coming from the man with the luxury apartment who uses the skyline as a nightlight."

"Nice place, right?"

"Oh, shut up, you just want to hear me say it. You're so mature… You always have been, though. Your success doesn't surprise me."

Megan's voice brought me back to reality. "I'm going to use the restroom, is that okay?"

"Of course, help yourself. It's right down the hall."

Immediately, my stomach sank. I remembered the passport on the shelf.

"Please, God, no," I whispered as I buried my head in the pillow.

Two minutes later, I heard the toilet and the sink run simultaneously. I braced myself for the impact while trying to stay calm.

Megan walked into the room half-naked with my passport in her left hand as she smacked it against her right hand.

"So, where are you headed?" Megan asked.

"What do you mean?"

"Cut the crap, no one just leaves their passport in their bathroom unless they plan on departing that same week."

"Okay, you got me. You caught me red-handed."

"I'm not mad. You can just tell me where you're headed."

"Nowhere," I said as I snatched the passport out of Megan's hands and walked to the bathroom. I turned the sink on and pretended to run soap through my palms.

"You're going somewhere, just tell me. Why does it matter?" I heard her yell from the bedroom.

"I needed it to declare unemployment. I don't have a job."

"Didn't you mention you received a severance?"

"Yeah, so?"

"Well, if you have a severance, you're not eligible for unemployment."

"Really?"

"Yeah, I'm an aspiring actress and a server, I'm practically the queen of unemployment."

I was running out of ways to distract the conversation, meanwhile, my white flag was practically hanging out of my back pocket.

And then, walking back into my bedroom, when I least expected it, my phone lit up with a text alert. I was a few feet away, but Megan and I could both read the size twelve font from a distance.

"This a friendly reminder for your flight scheduled tomorrow from Newark International Airport (EWR) to Istanbul Airport (IST)."

"What is this?" Megan lifted my screen and arched it as her facial expression went from cold to bright red blush.

I couldn't seem to make eye contact with Megan, as bad as I wanted to, I couldn't bring myself to look up.

"You're going to chase Azra?"

I shrugged my hands up in the air and sighed. "What do you want me to say? You suggested it, don't you remember?"

"What are you, a child? You have sex with me and don't tell me, even though I was the one who suggested it in the first place?"

"It's not that simple, Megan."

"Oh no, it actually is that simple. You just wanted to fuck me. You have this fantasy about my connection to Azra, and you were just using me. Admit it."

"That's not true; in fact I didn't even know I was going to see you that day."

"Oh, so you just randomly stumbled into my restaurant?"

"Yeah, that sounds about right."

"You know what, this was a mistake."

"Megan, come on, slow down. You handed me a note and you brought up Azra's cousin.

Okay, so what? I forgot to mention I was actually going. Why can't you be happy for me?"

"No, don't tell me to slow down. You're a loser, that's what you are. Oh, I'm so happy for you. You get the best of both worlds. You need to let Azra go, leave it in the past, where it belongs."

"Oh, I'm the loser, yeah, that's a good one."

"Just say it, I know what you're thinking."

"Well, at least I went for something. I made a name for myself. I didn't just stumble into this apartment."

"Oh, that's real nice. So you think because I'm working at a restaurant with a degree from NYU that I never went for anything? Wrong, I risked everything. My dream is to be an actress. Your dream is to find Azra and force her to love you."

My face went grey, and my stomach sank as we both stood there in silence for thirty seconds, a time that felt like an eternity but in reality, summed up our encounter.

"Look, Max, I didn't mean that. But I'm risking everything to get my SAG card. It might take me a little while, but don't compare me to this reverie you have of this life that never happened between you and Azra."

Megan's words cut like a knife, yet, in that moment, I sucked it up and asked her the question that weighed on my shoulders since the morning Azra left.

"Did Azra love me?"

Megan looked down and adjusted her pants to buy herself extra time. "I guess you need to go and find out for yourself, huh?"

"I guess so. Will you still be around when I get back?"

"Unless I get called to Hollywood, I'll be here in New York, hustling like I've always been. But now, I must leave. Good luck, Max."

Megan exited my room and I walked out to my balcony.

"New York, please be here when I get back."

I poured a glass of water from the kitchen sink, brushed my teeth, and went to bed.

Chapter 6: Chasing Azra

I set my alarm for 3:55 a.m. My flight was at 6:15, so I had just enough time to quickly shower, put some cereal in a bowl, and get to it. I wasn't a huge traveler, though I was lucky to have come from a family that showed me how to enjoy the finer things in life.

The shower water was cold, and I didn't have time to wait for the perfect temperature. I was already putting the shampoo and conditioner on my hair before my body was fully immersed. Then, a wave of anxiety, fear, and unknown overcame my body, and my stomach slipped into a dark place that only the moment could describe.

Eventually, the water did heat up, but by that time, I was already ready to get out and wash up. There were so many action items on my list, but, in reality, all I needed was my carry on, toothbrush, and headphones. Oh, and an Uber. I realized that there was more time than I had originally anticipated, so I put the television on in the living room.

"Italy is starting to see more cases of Covid-19 as new discoveries continue."

News of Covid-19 was everywhere, and the fear of a virus—one that you couldn't physically see—was a scary thought that I refused to fully process.

I turned the television off as quickly as possible. I was about to enter a country that wasn't necessarily taken from heaven's gates; the last thing I needed was to be reminded of a virus that was actively taking the lives of citizens in

Europe. So, instead, I walked to the lobby and waited for my car service.

"Hey, Max, early morning for you?" Edward asked. Edward was my doorman and front entrance security, not to mention a dear friend.

"I'll be out of town for a little bit. Hold the fort down for me yeah?"

"Well, hold on just a second then." Edward walked into the front desk drawer and grabbed a translucent white bag from the top shelf. "Here are three medical masks, I have a few extra, you can't find these anymore. Try to put these to good use."

"Thanks, I think?"

"I've got some business to take care of. See you when I get back?"

"I won't even ask you where you're headed, but yes, I'll see you when you get back."

Then, just as I was about to head out the door, I came two inches from slamming into a couple who were just returning from a night of fun and debauchery.

"Watch where you're going," the man who was most likely fifteen years my senior yelled.

"I tried, but I can't," I responded.

I entered the Uber like it was a getaway car and threw my headphones into a private meditation playlist.

I fell asleep but woke up naturally three or so minutes before I approached the gate at the airport.

"Here we are," the Uber driver yelled. "Safe flight."

"Thank you, sir, enjoy the day."

A feeling of doubt entered my bones. "What am I doing?" I said out loud.

But, as brave and fearless as I was, I still needed an iced coffee before I could think straight. That coffee was my sole motivation to get through the onboarding process, especially to make my way through security.

"Shoes, belts, phone, wallet. Everything out," TSA yelled.

As I was unbuckling my belt, a woman about ten years older than me caught my eye. We shared a moment—brief yet powerful. TSA proceeded to keep the line moving.

"Sir, sir, please, everything out of your pockets."

"Yes, sorry, I apologize."

"It's okay, let's keep it moving."

The woman was finished going through TSA, and she threw her hair back with her two hands as a guide to the back of her neck. She walked on through like she owned the airport, but by the looks of things, she most certainly didn't work for anyone—a self-made boss of some sort.

"Surprised all of you folks are still traveling."

"Have you seen fewer departures due to Covid-19?" I asked the TSA agent.

"Let's just say it's been very quiet around here. Stay safe, my friend."

I saw the Dunkin Donuts from the distance and raced there with my carry-on like I was chasing the flight. Funny how two things can be so close yet never touch.

The line at Dunkin was short in comparison to the city streets of New York. The service was naturally a little bit slower at the airport, ironically enough, as us travelers were in quite the time pinch.

The line started to advance, suddenly the man in front of me with his AirPods hanging off the side of his ear like jewelry decided to exit from the line. He was certainly in a rush, and I guess he decided that a soda on the plane would suffice. Fast forward to now, and it was me and the mysterious woman from the TSA security line.

"Seven dollars and twenty-nine cents, ma'am," the Dunkin counter associate requested.

The woman rushed through her purse, looking for cash, but it was sadly nowhere to be found. "I'm sorry, just give me a second. I'm so sorry, I would use Apple pay but my phone just ran out of battery."

"Take your time, ma'am, there's no rush."

"Excuse me, ma'am," I stepped in.

"I'm sorry, young man, now is not the time," the woman said as she briefly lifted her eyes to my level.

"No, I'm offering to pay. It's seriously no big deal. I can see you misplaced your cash. You were probably rushing this morning."

"Oh, that's sweet, but..."

"No, seriously, it's on me. It's the least I can do. Lord knows I could use some good karma."

"That's very sweet, are you sure?"

"I'm as sure as day."

"Do you do this for all the women you meet?"

85

"Do you forget to carry cash at every Dunkin Donuts?"

The woman laughed and put her hand on my forearm. "You're very funny, and the answer is no, for your information. Besides, cash is very archaic. Where are you headed?"

I raised my index finger as I ordered my iced coffee and handed over another ten-dollar bill. "Turkey. Istanbul, to be exact. And yourself?"

"No kidding. Same here. And where are you staying?"

"Big airport, small world. The Four Seasons Hotel at the Bosphorus."

"Are you stalking me or something?"

"It sounds like you may be staying there as well?"

"Yeah, it sounds like we are also on the same flight. So, tell you what, why don't we exchange Instagram handles, and when we arrive, you can message me and see if I'm not busy with work. I never asked, what brings you to Istanbul?"

"Oh, it's a long story, best to be shared with a glass of wine, maybe? How about yourself?"

"You had me at wine. And my baby stepbrother is a professional basketball player in Istanbul. Doesn't see the court much, but I'm not really visiting to watch him play. He's a little homesick, as I'm sure you could imagine. But regardless, you had me at wine."

"I take your name is Sonya, you know, by your Instagram name?" Sonya had finished typing it in simultaneously as we chatted.

"Very smart. You're doing well so far," Sonya sarcastically assured me.

"Well, Sonya, I will see you when we land, perhaps?"

"See you when we land, I hope," she winked.

As unfortunate as some of the events in my life came to be, there was so much luck associated with my name. Meeting a woman in line at a Dunkin Donuts is not a test of my skill or 'game' but rather a testament of my timing. I shook my iced coffee slowly yet steadily and found a seat far away from where Sonya settled in. I threw on a podcast titled "Master your finances," mainly because it passed the time more than anything else.

Sonya glanced at me from across the row of chairs. I smiled back, but I didn't want to seem obsessive. I would let her come to me if it was fated to happen. I started to get restless, and with fifty minutes before boarding, I decided to go to the bookstore and look for an interesting read. I had gone through most of my downloaded podcasts, and I needed to save some the music for the second leg of my flight. On a nine-hour flight, you develop a strategy—any big-time traveler knows that.

"Hey, sir, can I help you?" the bookstore attendant asked.

"Yeah, I think you can. I'm taking a long flight overseas, and I could use an inspirational read. Got anything that you think would pique my interest?"

"Do you want my personal opinion?"

"Sure, go for it."

"I recently read an absolutely intriguing book. It's titled: 'Sum: Forty Tales from the Afterlives,' by David Eagleman."

"Any good?"

"It's quite spectacular, honestly."

"I'll take it then."

"Yeah?"

"Yeah, why not?"

"Okay then. Your total will be 39.99, how would you like to pay?"

"I'll use my card. I tell you what, you're a great salesperson. I didn't think I would be spending forty dollars on a book for my flight, but here I am."

"I didn't think I would have an English degree from Babson College and be working at an airport bookstore."

"Well, take care," I said.

"Have a nice flight."

I put my headphones back in for the next few minutes until we boarded, and when I finally got on a plane, it really started to hit me. "Wow I'm really doing this," I whispered as I sat down.

"This is flight 204 from Newark International Airport to Istanbul Airport in Turkey. Thank you for flying on Turkish Airlines."

I put my seatbelt on and laid back for the first hour of the flight. Before the wheels even left the ground, I fell into a deep sleep. Luckily for me, the older woman next to me was also sleeping, and it just felt right to follow her lead. I woke up sporadically with drool running down the side of my cheeks. It reminded me of the long days and sleepless nights at the library when I was completing my MBA. The nostalgia of college brought me back to even simpler times with Azra; the little things like going to our favorite Chinese place, arguing over politics, and city planning. Azra was such a nerd, and so was I. Neither of us were born in Manhattan, yet we still considered ourselves true New Yorkers. I dreamed of the discussions we had on the best museums and best neighborhoods the city had to offer. I reminisced about the arguments we got into.

"Max, would you say I'm more of a 'Brooklyn in the summer' or 'Upper East Side in the winter' kind of gal?"

"How about an East Village gal? I mean, that's where we live, right? Why do you ask?"

"Oh, no reason."

"You can tell me."

"A resident I work with said I looked like a Brooklyn in the summer kind of gal, that's all."

"What does that even mean?"

"I'm not sure. I told him I was more Upper East Side in the winter. I figured you would like that response."

"I mean, why is he asking these types of questions? Who is this guy again?"

"He's a resident at the hospital. What, are you jealous or something?"

"No, why would I be jealous?"

"I don't think you are, it's just that—"

"Just what? Just say it."

"Oh, I wasn't sure if you were intimidated because he's a doctor and—"

"And, what? I aspire to work in finance. Is my future six-figure salary not good enough? Do you insist I go back to school for four more years, huh? Maybe I can get a second bachelor's degree in pre-med, and the government can pay for my food and recreation?"

"I don't assume you're jealous, but it's okay to get jealous."

"Oh yeah, so now you're saying it's okay for me to be jealous because you're jealous of me from time to time?"

"Yeah, that's exactly what I'm saying."

"Well, you shouldn't be jealous. It's unhealthy; you know that, right? Besides, when do you ever get jealous of me? No girls talk to me besides you."

"What about Megan?"

"Megan? Megan, as in your Megan?"

"What other Megan would I be referring to?"

I laughed. First, the smirking started slow, but eventually, the laughs grew louder and louder until Azra started laughing herself.

"So, you're saying you're jealous of Megan and me when we talk, even though you're always with us and listen to every conversation?"

"She looks at you differently than most girls, that's all. She's hooked up with you, she probably likes you."

"That's crazy."

Except when I think back on it, it really wasn't crazy at all. It made perfect sense. The flirtatious relationship that Megan and I had was an escape from the worlds that consumed us. Towards the end of college, our commitments were similar. Megan had pursued acting, and I was finishing up certifications so I could have a successful and lucrative career in the finance world. There was no looking back for either of us, and I think that's what we craved in one another. Azra was mostly worry-free. She had a drive that was unparalleled, but the level of momentum in her passions was less significant than Megan and me. Still, she had every right to be jealous, and it wasn't until that vague dream or memory of some sorts that I was finally able to recognize it.

"Hey…" Sonya nudged me as I fidgeted in my seat.

"Hi, I'm sorry. Hey, what's up?"

"Hey, I was just wondering if maybe in an hour you wanted to sit with me up in first class?"

"Wait, you have a seat in first class?"

"I actually have two seats. I don't like sitting next to strangers."

"I'm glad you don't view me as a stranger."

"You're fine. Just let me know."

"Wait, should I just come now?"

"I have some work to do on my laptop. Give me an hour and tell the flight attendant that you want to head over."

"Okay, thank you," I said.

"And let me know what you think about that book. I've read it myself."

My face turned bright red as saliva dripped down the side of my lip, a result of my nap just minutes before. I had never considered myself a big reader, but then again, I wasn't much of a traveler, either.

"Yeah, it's heating up," I said.

Sonya moved back to her seat, and I poured the complimentary Coca-Cola that the flight attendant must have left on the tray in front of my seat. I buried my mind in the book, reading every detail with such engagement and interest. The author had hooked me in like a fish looking for more bait. With every page I turned, I mentally began to crave more. I read and read, and before I knew it, I was halfway through the story.

"Attention, this is your pilot. I hope you are enjoying your flight. We are expected to arrive on time to Istanbul, Turkey—our final destination. Thank you once again for flying Turkish Airlines."

Sonya looked up at me from the front of the plane and moved her chin ever so subtly, and I knew to get up and make my way towards her seat.

"Am I allowed to get up during the flight like this?"

"Well, you're up now, so sit down and get ready to drink with me," Sonya demanded.

"Oh, we're drinking?" I questioned myself and every decision that I had made up until this point.

"We aren't just drinking, we're drinking to forget," Sonya reminded me.

"Cheers to Turkey?" I asked.

"Happy Turkey day," Sonya joked.

"Happy Turkey day," I added. "Cheers."

"So, some book, huh?" Sonya said.

"I'm sorry, come again?"

"The book, you know the one you had with you when I came over to your seat." Sonya leaned in. "It really makes you think, right?"

"Oh yeah. It sure does."

The truth was, "I was relieved that I had actually read the book, instead of just skimming it for its key points to make conversation, which had been my plan."

"So, Max, tell me, why are you visiting? I don't think we got that far."

"Well, this is a pleasant surprise, I thought when you asked me for my Instagram it was more of a friendly invitation to fuck off."

"Shhh, watch your language, we're on an airplane," Sonya said as she poured me a glass of God knows what.

"Are you sure it's okay to drink here?"

"Of course, honey. Sounds like you don't travel much, huh?"

"I don't travel too often. I've always had opportunities with work—I'm in finance, by the way. And in my early twenties, I had this girlfriend, Azra, who I lived with, and who I was very happy with in New York. Actually, that's why I'm visiting, to hopefully see Azra."

"Aww, that's so cute," Sonya said as she made a frowning face with her lips, just enough to make a young man weak in the heart. Sonya was gorgeous, and it wasn't just her sophisticated style and bright white teeth; it was her mannerisms and confidence in how she spoke. Most older women would be shy around a younger man, blaming it on some irrational fear or insecurity that they weren't young or pretty enough. But I truly believe that Sonya, who couldn't have been a day under forty, believed she was twenty-four, and that thought became a credence of her surroundings and a reflection of those that came under her aura.

"Cute?" I asked.

"How old are you?" Sonya shot back.

"I'm twenty-eight."

"So, you're visiting an ex-girlfriend who's from Turkey. Oh, I'm not sure if she ever deserved you."

"What do you mean by that?"

"Well, you're traveling halfway across the globe in hope of maybe, possibly meeting your ex-girlfriend. Istanbul is a big city. Do you think you're going to run into her?"

"It's not even about finding her."

Sonya took another sip of her drink. This time, slowly, and given the length of the flight, it was clear there was no rush. "What's it about then?"

"Understanding why she left. Understanding who she is. Understanding where she's from."

"Oh, that's very romantic, but even more so, quite impressive."

"I just want to know I gave everything, and then—"

Sonya cut me off, "And then you can say goodbye, for good?"

"Yeah, how'd you know?"

"I'm divorced, sweetheart. I feel naked without my ring. Trust me, it was quite a nice piece of jewelry, but it's no longer mine."

"If you don't mind me asking, how did that end? Or maybe, how did it happen?"

"We met at a bar in Manhattan. My friend was into his friend, and I don't think either of us wanted to be there. It was a hot afternoon in July, and my friend had just gotten broken up with."

"You met at a bar. I feel like so many couples meet at bars, yet almost none of them admit it."

"Yep, I was supposed to be in the Hamptons, but my friend Grace was my connect to the Amagansett pool house where we had planned on staying. We were twenty-four, and her boyfriend at the time was thirty-two. He came from money, but he was also a successful real estate agent."

"So, it's summer in NYC, and you take your friend out to get her mind off a breakup, yet you end up meeting your future, now ex, husband?"

"That's correct. Greg."

"Greg?"

"His name is Greg."

"What was Greg doing at the time? When you first met?"

"Greg was the perfect catch. He was twenty-nine, well-spoken, attractive, I mean he looked like he was twenty-three, and even now, he looks like the age he was when I first met him."

"What was his story?"

"He worked in advertising. He was at a big company, but I remember one of the first things he said to me, 'I'll have my own business by thirty.'"

"Wow, very ambitious." And, in some ways, it opened my thoughts to why I wasn't starting my own business—personal consulting, at the very least.

"I was doing well, but I think I was attracted to losers at the time. I had never met someone with energy and drive like Greg."

"So, you started dating?"

"Yes, it started casual with coffee. And then gradually it led to dinners, and before you knew it, we were staying over at each other apartments and cuddling, watching football in the fall."

"Sounds like a beautiful relationship."

"It was, he was perfect, and I think in some ways, I was perfect for him."

"So, then, if you don't mind me asking…"

"Of course, I don't mind. Eventually, we moved in together. I agreed to a two-bedroom apartment, even though it was very expensive and not so practical. But, because Greg had his own business, he needed a room for his home office."

"Sounds like Greg had a good plan, but those NYC two bedrooms are not cheap."

"We were living in Tribeca, one of the more expensive neighborhoods in the city."

"I know Tribeca, go on."

"So, we got married a year after dating. Greg's marketing business took off. He was always on a call, and if he wasn't on a call, he was on a golf course in Westchester or Long Island. It seemed like I had hit the lottery."

"Life was good, you would say?"

"It was good, and work was rewarding for me. I was always more passionate about my hobbies. You know, swimming, yoga, or just wine night with my girlfriends. Greg's dreams, in some ways, allowed me to pursue my happiness in a very ironic way, which in return felt like I was also living a dream. I was genuinely happy."

"So? I now need to know, what happened? I'm invested."

"Well, I think the reason Greg's business was such a success was because his only two employees were trusted colleagues from his old firm. But then one afternoon, everything changed."

"Keep going; if you feel comfortable, that is."

"So, Greg told me he was having a company meeting at the apartment and he wanted me to be there to welcome the two new employees. I obviously agreed and prepared snacks and drinks, everything a supporting wife would do for her man."

"So, this was a company all-hands, at your apartment?"

"Yeah, all five employees. When the first new hire walked in, I was relieved. It was an older man with years of experience. He was kind and his wife joined him at the meeting. She was incredibly sweet and very genuine and supportive to me."

"But the other hire?" I took a deep sip from the drink that Sonya had poured for me just a few minutes prior.

"The other hire was a cute and petite twenty-two-year-old student. She had almost no work experience but was obtaining her master's from Columbia Business school—"

"That's where I got my MBA."

Sonya stared at me, obviously not appreciative of my interruption.

"Sorry, continue," I said.

"Her name was Kristin, and they all called her K.J., her last name was Johnson... real original."

"So, she was an intern?"

"Oh no, she was a full-time employee, and they were paying her a lot. That's when I started to get curious, yet, I stayed out of it. It wasn't my place."

"But?"

Sonya cut me off, "Like I said, it wasn't my place."

"Fair enough."

"So," Sonya grabbed her drink and twisted it like a teacup in her palms. "About six months later, I came home one Friday afternoon early from the Hamptons. I didn't feel the need to let my husband know because I assumed he was at work; I guess I didn't realize work that day would be him and K.J. alone in the home office."

"So, this twenty-two-year-old employee who you barely knew was just casually handling business calls with your husband and no one else, just to be clear?"

"Just the two of them. So, I went inside to the hallway closet and grabbed the door so my heels halted on the wooden floor. I slide them off just quickly enough to listen in."

"But then?"

"But then I heard the sound of silence, the most painful sound of all."

"You reacted, right?"

"Yes, in some way, I reacted. But I think the silence scared me, so instead of finding the answer to the question I refused to ask, I yelled his name."

"You wanted to give him a chance to stop what he was doing, so If he was guilty, you could still save the marriage."

"You're very mature for your age, you know that? Has anyone ever told you that?"

In some ways, I was flattered, but really, I was reminded of how almost no one had ever noticed that truth about me. All of my accomplishments and accolades, much like Sonya, were celebrated alone.

"That's the first time I've been told that."

Sonya shrugged. "Well, anyway, Greg paused for a few seconds, actually, it was more like five. But then, he finally spoke up."

"What did he say?"

"Honey...are you home?"

"What did you think?"

"At the time, I was relieved, but for eight years after, I never went to bed without wondering what happened in those five seconds."

"How did you let the girl get away with it, you know, Kristin?"

"It wasn't her battle."

"What do you mean it wasn't her battle?"

"If it wasn't Kristin, it would have been someone else. She was just the unfortunate scapegoat of our story."

"So, the marriage?" I asked. I avoided eye contact; it made sense to tread carefully.

"I found out that he did have an affair with Kristin but not until years later. But, by that time, the wounds had already happened, and the scars had already healed."

"You're so brave, I don't think I could have dealt with that."

"Towards the end, there were so many signs. The business was failing, I saw the bank statements, we downsized apartments, he gained weight, he was coming home drunk, and our sex life was practically non-existent."

"Did he ever confess to it?"

"Luckily for me, I could sense the desperation in Greg. I knew it was a sinking ship. So, in those years, I got my law degree and made sure I protected myself when he did decide to confess and admit his infidelities."

"You savage, you. I love that."

"I wasn't mad about Kristin; I was mad about who he pretended to be around me, mad about the years he stole from me."

I then started to think about the years I lost thinking about Azra. After she left, everything always reminded me of her. Even the small things—the glass of water, the way the shower made me feel before work when the sun was still rising. Everything. And even though I felt bad for Sonya, I began to feel even more sorry for myself.

"You won in the long run," I proclaimed.

"Let's not get carried away. You know the author in that book you were reading has this mesmerizing idea. He says, 'There are three deaths: The first is when the body ceases to function.'"

"That was the five second silence before your husband's response?"

"Correct. The second is when the body is consigned to the grave."

"That's when you began going back to law school. You were mentally already taking him away."

"Correct. The third is that moment, sometime in the future, when your name is spoken for the last time."

"Wait, he isn't, you know?"

"Dead? Oh, dear God, no. Well, to me maybe, but I know he is doing just fine. He landed on his feet. Still, the day I stopped loving him, well, let's just say that destroyed him." Sonya grinned. Her half smile was deceiving yet moving and quite profound.

I should have smiled back, but Sonya's explanation of death and romantic love frightened me. I feared the worst—what if Azra had felt love for me for the last time? What would that say about me, and why did I deserve such a tragic ending if I was the one chasing her?

"Is it okay if I rest on your shoulders now? Would you mind?" Sonya asked, interrupting my thoughts.

"No, no, of course, rest, of course."

Sonya laid her lips right below my ear and breathed through her nose as I held her head and gently rubbed the back of her neck. For the first time in a few years, we both found someone equally as broken yet so elegantly put back together. For Sonya, it brought her peace, but for me, it was frustrating, fueling my passion for the trip even more. We both closed our eyes and let the rest of the flight take care of itself.

"Attention all flight attendants and passengers, flight 204 is about a half-hour out. At this time, we ask all passengers and crew members to remain seated, if possible, for the duration of the flight. Once again, we want to take this time to thank you for flying with Turkish Airlines. Have a safe trip."

I looked out of the window as Sonya rested on my shoulders. I wanted to adjust my back and crack my neck, but she was resting so peacefully, it would have been a crime to wake her before we landed.

A moment later, Sonya lifted her face. "Have we landed?"

"Almost. The pilot just made an announcement." I looked down at my Rolex watch that I'd been meaning to fix for years. "About twenty minutes out," I followed up.

"Wow, quick flight," Sonya added before falling back into her dreams.

"Quick flight," I said to myself.

I glanced over to the tray of liquor and cups on the drop-down plastic that served as a makeshift counter. I eyed the glass of water, but this time it was in the form of a disposable cup. I hadn't even arrived in Istanbul yet Azra was still sending me signs from our past. I was relieved because I knew I would see her soon.

"How long was I out?"

"Oh, only a few minutes. You're fine."

"Oh, wow, it felt like I slept a whole night. I feel refreshed."

"That makes one of us," I whispered.

"Would you like to split a cab? After all, we're staying at the same resort."

"Oh, I really shouldn't," I said. "I don't want to hold you back. I'm sure you have a lot of things you want to do. I don't want to be a distraction."

"Oh, don't be silly. It would be foolish for us to part ways after coming this far. Plus, I could use some protection. You seem like a strong young man. Do you work out?"

What started as an intimate and deep conversation immediately turned to heavy flirting. You could smell the alcohol on Sonya's breath. It wasn't attractive, but who was I to judge a divorced middle-aged woman on an international flight?

"Yeah, unfortunately, I spend most of my alone time in the gym."

Sonya smiled, and I understood—that's what every middle-aged woman wanted to hear. Who wouldn't want a younger man who lifted weights five days a week? If only Sonya knew how intense my workouts really were. They were far from healthy; they were angry and motivated by pain. The same pain that brought me to another country during the development of a global deadly pandemic.

On the surface, I was normal. A well-mannered, respectful, nicely dressed young man in his late twenties, who partially benefitted from white privilege, who had a heartbreak that taught him tough lessons at a relatively young age. I had a babyface, so it was no surprise that older women tended to view me as inexperienced or potentially even immature. But those who knew me would say I was far from that. I chose to use this to my advantage, sure—use me as a project. Try and put me back together. I may have been roughed up, but my mentality was always far from broken. Still, I came across as fragile to women, especially older lovers, and in some ways, that was my sick and twisted game.

"I don't trust Uber here, so I think it's best if we hop in a more organized car service. Is that okay with you?"

At this point, I didn't even know what to say, but a part of me was relieved that I had someone with me who was well-traveled with a good head on her shoulders. I didn't want to admit it, but I was extremely grateful.

"Thank you," I said softly.

"What's that, sweetheart?"

"Thank you…for looking out for me. I do appreciate it. Oh, and the drinks."

"Oh, you're just happy you got me drunk."

"Wait, you don't think that, do you?"

"Honey, I'm kidding. I'm glad we had a good time. Here, this looks like a proper vehicle for us."

"Sonya, be careful," I said as I moved her away from the aggressive black truck that was certainly not in the hospitality and service business.

"Well, this is certainly not Soho or Tribeca."

"Here, I think we got one," I said as I held Sonya close to my hip.

"Ride, yes, you need?"

"Oh, thank you so much. You're a true lifesaver," Sonya added as she dragged me in the car. "Come, come, honey."

I stepped in and triple-checked my phone, wallet, and keys. Even though I was irresponsible at times, I had never lost or misplaced my cell phone or credit cards; I couldn't help but let my anxiety creep into my bloodline.

"You have everything, make sure, double-check."

"Just relax, honey. We are fine."

"You pay lira. How much? Thirty-five dollars from America, you have, yes?" the driver asked.

"That's it?" I looked at Sonya. "Wait, does he know where we're going?"

"I just handed him the address on paper. I like to be prepared, just in case."

I was impressed by Sonya's organization despite her heavy buzz. But the truth was, I would have probably been lost without her.

"Four Seasons Hotel, Bosphorus, okay?"

"Yes, yes, I see, I go there," the driver assured me.

"You go there?"

"Yes, I go there. You pay me five extra, I get you there quicker."

I handed the driver a folded ten-dollar bill. "Keep it, sir."

105

"Thank you very, very much, thank you so much. Very nice, thank you."

"So," Sonya added. "What would you like to do?"

"What do you mean?" I pretended to look puzzled, but my confusion was forced, to put it nicely.

"You're not going to help me get settled. I might need help with my luggage."

"Oh, I'm sure there will be a bellhop or a doorman. You will be fine."

Sonya gave me the silent treatment for the last fifteen minutes of the ride to the resort, and rightfully so. I deserved some sort of consequence for how I led her on. This was my routine. I had been here before, even though I acted innocent and perhaps wholesome.

We walked in together and were met by the hotel front desk.

"Welcome to Four Seasons Hotel at the Bosphorus. I'm Eren. How can I help you?"

"Check-in?" Sonya asked.

"Same here," I added.

Sonya behaved like we were strangers.

After checking our reservations, Eren said, "Okay, you two are all set."

"Okay, thank you, sweetheart," Sonya added. "Is there anyone to help me with my bags?"

The front desk agent bit his upper lip. "Oh, I'm afraid our porter went home sick. But the good news is we have baggage carousels that can help out."

106

I looked at Sonya and I saw right through her and everything that she had been through, and I couldn't resist her beauty.

"Sonya, let me help."

I quickly grabbed as many bags as I could hold, and the veins of my forearms popped out as her eyes made their way to my arms.

Sonya smiled. "Thanks, honey."

I nodded at the front desk agent and proceeded to make my way to the elevator, completely disregarding my bags that dragged slowly behind me on the carousel.

We stayed quiet in the elevator. It was just us two, and we both knew what we were thinking. But, when we finally started moving up, things became more normal between us.

"Looks like I'm one floor up; that's convenient."

"That's, well, perfect," Sonya reassured me.

"Well, this is us," I said.

Sonya quickly swiped her card to her room. "Ugh, thank God," she said as she threw her carry-on bag onto the queen mattress and took her knapsack into the bathroom. "Just give me a minute."

I pretended to look busy, but in reality, the anticipation of Sonya walking out of the bathroom in a bathing suit was enough to make a grown man weak in the knees. So, I stayed put.

Then, the door started to click; she was quick and true to her word. Sonya came out of the bathroom with just a robe and hotel slippers on.

"I feel brand new," Sonya announced.

"You look, comfortable, I think."

"You think? Yes, well I am."

"I better get going. Have to drop my things off."

Sonya then stared at me and smiled. Instinctively, I smiled back, not so much because I wanted to, but more out of fear of creating an awkward scenario. Next thing I knew, Sonya unraveled the belt that held in her thin yet crisp and durable robe. She held it out for a few seconds before ultimately letting it fall to the floor.

Many men would have been lost in the moment, but I was thinking of the water that fell from the shower head as Azra left me for the last time. I then thought of the first time Azra let me hold her and how Megan joined in. My sexual experiences were so elevated that I couldn't enjoy a beautiful middle-aged woman with the most natural features a man under thirty had ever witnessed.

I looked at her and said, "Wow."

"This is your reward for keeping me company," Sonya told me. "Here, it's for you."

Sonya was about five foot seven but appeared taller. Her hair was natural but had grey strands that complimented her very subtle wrinkles. Her boobs were natural, big and perky. They seemed too perfect for anyone, let alone a woman in her mid-forties. Her butt was as round and toned as a supermodel on the beach, the natural shape was eye opening and even jaw dropping.

"Grab my ass," she demanded.

I did what I was told.

"Now lay me down on this bed and do whatever you want to me. But before you please me, kiss my neck and make me beg for it."

I didn't hesitate this time or even think of Azra. There wouldn't be a second chance with Sonya. Even though we were from the same city, there would be no future night of casual drinks. This was the opportunity, and I took it.

We made love for at least an hour, and the high was high but the come down was one of the worst fallouts I had ever experienced. Sonya was beautiful, but my regret immediately overtook the endorphins formed from her natural aura and appeal. My stomach sank. If I was looking for sex, well, I had a lot of it in New York. That's not why I flew halfway around the world. I came here for the love of my life, Azra. If I saw her, what would I say? By not telling her about Sonya, I would be lying, but there's no way I could have that conversation. "Hey, Azra, I'm glad I tracked you down, I just had hot sex with a divorced, middle-aged woman. How have you been?" I couldn't stay mad at Azra if my behavior was this erratic and volatile, and at this point, it would just be easier to be a tourist. Yet, I didn't go back to my room. I loved the comfort of Sonya's body, the smell of her hair, and the taste of her lips. Her voice soothed my confused and cold soul. Her toes tickled my ankles, a feeling you didn't know you missed until you felt it again. Despite this, I was able to resist the euphoria.

"I better get going," I said as I rummaged for my briefs, pants, and socks.

"Hit and run?" Sonya said as she lunged for a mini water bottle that was tucked under the nightstand.

I looked at Sonya but didn't say anything for about a minute. My hesitation said it all. I was bad at being the bad guy.

"Okay, if that's how it's going to be."

"Unfortunately, it has to be this way. See you around, Sonya."

I grabbed my luggage and made my way through the elevator. I buried my face in the palm of my hands.

"Why?" I shouted as I punched my fists together. "Why do I have to always make things so complicated for myself?"

The elevator opened on my floor, and I entered the four-digit pin to the door that was sent to my email folder upon arrival. The layout, for the most part, was similar to Sonya's. Basic television, round cups of water with buckets for ice. There was even a crisp bi-folded note with my name on it, the ink practically melting off the stationery.

"Max, enjoy your stay, and welcome to Istanbul. I would personally recommend 16 roof for dinner." - Front Desk

"Well, this is either coincidence or fate," I said out loud, realizing 16 roof was the same restaurant Megan told me about, where I might be able to find Azra's cousin.

I took my iPhone out of my pocket and searched: 16 roof. It seemed touristy, but ultimately, it looked fun. I needed to get away from the hotel, away from Sonya. Plus, I had to remember why I was in Turkey in the first place: to find Azra, and if I wasn't able to, well, at least I'd know where she came from.

I went down to the front desk.

"How can we help you, Max?"

"Is there a car service the hotel would recommend?"

"Sure, right away. And where are you headed tonight?" the agent asked.

"I think I'm going to try and hit 16 roof. I've heard good things."

Some of the agents stared and laughed with each other.

"What's so funny?" I asked as I caught on.

"No, no, it's just that 16 roof is where all the tourists go. You'll fit right in."

"Well, after all, I am a tourist."

The car was there within minutes, and I hopped in like I was the son of the Vice President of the United States.

"16 roof," I said.

"Sure thing," the driver quickly replied.

It seemed that Ubers and private car services were becoming a popular theme of my travels.

"Do you have a mask?" the driver asked.

I flashed it like a badge.

Before I left, I had started seeing more men and women wear masks in Manhattan. The airports were about fifteen percent masked, but even then, you could tell that most residents were starting to take this virus seriously. The virus was the reason I lost my job, but I was an early victim.

If anything, my former employer did me a favor. Little had I known I was sleeping on a sinking ship for years—but more on that later.

I got comfortable in the back of the cab, and this time, I kept my mouth shut. The ride was quick and convenient from where I was located. As I gazed out the window at the sights of this new place, I felt more alive than I had in years. Sure, Manhattan was buzzing with action and excitement every night, but visiting another country was liberating. I had nothing to lose and everything to gain.

"Here you are, sir."

"That was quick."

"Well, it's a tourist attraction, not far from anything."

"Everyone keeps saying that."

"Everyone says it because it's true."

"A tourist I will be then."

I got to the lobby of the building and asked for the rooftop. The tall man at the front door had asked for my passport for ID, and of course, I had left it back in my room. So, like any tourist, naturally, I panicked.

"Passport?" I patted my pockets and hoped that something would appear, knowing very well I only had my New York State ID card.

"Yes, quick, yes, ID."

My face turned red before any excuse or counteroffer could leave my lips.

"Do you think you could make an exception?"

Then, the bouncer burst out in laughter. "Oh, you should have seen your face. Priceless,

priceless. You Americans are too much. Go, go, go, quick."

"Thank you, thank you," I said.

I entered the lobby elevator and adjusted my clothes.

"Rooftop?" the elevator attendant asked.

"Yes, restaurant please."

"Just visiting? From America?"

"Yes, how does everyone know that?"

"Don't take it personally, your smile says it all. It's okay. You look happy to be here. Expecting someone?"

"Yeah, sort of. Well, not expecting, hoping, maybe?"

"Doesn't hurt to hope, yes?"

"Doesn't hurt to hope, doesn't hurt to hope," I repeated a few times, even as I exited the elevator. "Doesn't hurt to hope," I reminded myself one last time.

The music from the narrow hallway led to a small, dense dance floor, which opened for me like I was Moses parting the red sea.

"Buy me a drink," a young woman demanded. She seemed to be older than twenty-one but most certainly younger than me.

"Uhm, can I get a minute, please?" I requested. I stood my ground; there was something so unsettling about being a solo traveler, let alone an out-of-place tourist.

"Ask for Raki," the young woman said. "Raki for me and my friends."

"Three," I demanded from the bartender. "Raki, right?" I reiterated.

"Yes, correct. Are you American?"

"Is it that obvious?"

"You are very handsome, that's all."

"Oh, thank you. I'm looking for someone. But thank you, enjoy your night and enjoy your drink."

"Okay, take care," the young woman said as she took out her iPhone to check her makeup.

"Well, she got over me quickly," I chuckled to myself.

I left a few extra dollars for the bartender. She was tall, blonde, and skinny, but not unhealthily thin; she had the type of physique that showed her off well.

"Thank you, baby," she said.

"Hey!" I caught her attention. "Hey, just one second. Sorry, I know you're busy, but is Demir here? Is he working today by any chance?"

"You know Demir?"

"Well, technically, no. I need to ask him about Azra."

"You know Azra?" the bartender asked.

"How do *you* know Azra?" I shot back at her.

"Baby, it's busy here. Hold on, I'll see if I can find Demir. Last time I checked, he was eating, but I'll see what I can do."

I threw five US dollars down on the bar and she looked at me and swayed her hips. So, out of desperation, I threw another five-dollar bill on top.

She picked up the fresh tip. "I'll go get Demir. Actually, follow me."

The bartender grabbed my hand as her long blonde locks guided me like a rope through the jungle. I dodged men twice my size with drinks at my chin swaying left to right in hopes of making my way to Demir. My stomach sank and my heart pounded. I was close yet so far away from finding the final clue, the final step, the final answer. A ball of sweat developed under my arms and I was close to shutting down completely.

"Hello, boss, this young man is here to see you."

I looked on like a young fan at a baseball game who was waiting to get his favorite slugger's autograph. After all, I was just an outsider looking in.

"And who is this you bring me?" Demir asked.

"When I was serving him, he mentioned your name and Azra."

Demir stepped up from his seat and placed his napkin down on the chair. "Follow me, let's talk."

So, I did what any desperate twenty-eight-year-old would do who was placed in my situation. I followed the man to wherever it was he wanted to take me. I was at his disposal.

"Come, sit down, you are my guest. Do you need anything?"

"Just a water, maybe?"

"Water, yes, of course. Water." Demir snapped his fingers and two servers stopped what they were doing and immediately catered to our table.

They filled the glass, and just as the liquid maxed out, I was drawn back, once again, to the early morning all those years ago that Azra left. The phone call. The shower, but mostly, the pain of the time that I couldn't control.

"Thank you," I told the servers. Their smiles were fake, superficial, but enough to set a positive tempo at the club.

"Drink, drink then," Demir said.

I took a sip and swallowed it quickly.

"Do you know who I am?"

"Yes, yes, I do."

"But I didn't even introduce myself."

"Right, but you said 'Azra'. In some ways, I was expecting to hear from you."

"But we never—"

I was immediately cut off by Demir. "I know we never met, but I heard a lot about you."

My throat started to close up. "Good things, I hope?" I doubted myself but felt my gut point me towards the good times Azra and I shared together.

"Great things, Max. Great things."

I took another sip of water. "I came here not so much in search of her, but in the search and understanding of where she was from, how she grew up."

"Well, you have come to the right place," Demir said. "You know what, follow me."

Leaving this time was way easier after I had earned the respect of Demir. I felt free and confident, even maybe a bit more like myself again. Demir took me to a reserved room where tables of beautiful women and successful men in suits were smoking cigars and drinking fancy bottles of liquor. There was old and sophisticated urban artwork on the wall, and every server was a

116

beautiful woman who was just as happy to be there as the men they served, despite their fake smiles.

"You like?" Demir asked.

"I think so, yes, I do." I hesitated but looked at Demir for approval.

"It's okay, it's just me, you can be honest."

"Yes, I like a lot. So, you manage this place?"

"Manage? Max, tell me, do I look like a man who works for another man?"

"Oh, I just thought this was your job?"

"Well, you're right. It is my job. I own this place."

Demir was certainly a man of influence, at least in his inner circle. I, for one, was an unemployed, overly emotional boy who had traveled halfway around the world looking for answers to questions that should have been asked many moons ago.

"Well, anyway, thank you for taking some time to meet with me."

"Of course. Thank you for making the trip to Turkey. You came alone?"

"Yes, I decided this was a trip I needed to take alone."

Demir burst out laughing. "So, you came all the way from America, during what could be an international health crisis, because of your college girlfriend?"

I couldn't believe what I was hearing. I had a great sense of humor, sure, but the last thing I wanted was for anyone to look at me like I was a joke.

"Maybe I should go. I think coming here was a mistake. Thank you for meeting with me," I said coldly as I gathered myself to exit.

There's something about silence; as ironic as it may be, it has a sound.

"Hey, kid, come back here."

Demir was at least ten years older than me. He was probably in his late thirties, but he looked like he was in his early forties. He an intimidating look, yet his demeanor was calm. Demir called over another server. She couldn't have been a day over twenty-two and signaled for two cigars. He poured a fresh drink as his Cuban rested on his lower lip like a retired man swaying in his poolside hammock.

"For me?" I motioned with my body language.

"Yes, sit down. Let's talk," Demir reassured me.

Immediately, we talked about Azra. We discussed her youth, her childhood, her friends, family, hobbies, interests. The clock rolled its hours over as the hands of time struck midnight, yet it still felt early. We continued to drink, talking about the cutthroat industry of NYC finance and everything that came along with it. As different as we were, many parts of our lives aligned, and our conversation became more fluent. But eventually, midnight became 1:00 a.m., and 1:00 a.m. became 1:30 a.m. I knew the conversation eventually had to end at some point or another. The DJ slowed his music down, and a lull in the conversation developed.

"Max, why are you really here?"

"What do you mean?"

"You can be real with me, we had a good time tonight, right? A few drinks, yes?"

I moved my chair closer to Demir. I made sure he could hear me loud and clear. "I came here for one reason, to see Azra."

"Why don't I believe that?"

"I think you're choosing not to believe it, and I can't seem to figure out why."

"It's just, I don't understand who would travel across the world for someone they used to date in college? I just don't see it adding up. You're a smart kid, a numbers guy of some sorts, you wouldn't do that." Demir then shook his glass of ice that became crushed glacier like the snow that was pushed up against the curb during a New York City winter storm.

"I don't know what to tell you. I'm here for Azra."

I took one last sip of my drink and put the last of my cigar out in the ashtray.

"Don't worry. If you won't tell me where Azra is, I'll find her myself."

Demir leaned in and switched his body language when he saw my level of intent to leave had risen. "Max, I have something to tell you."

"What? Is it that I'm an idiot, or let me guess, I should grow up? You know what, don't tell me how to live my life. You're not my boss."

"No, Max, that's not it."

"Then what is it?"

119

"I'm afraid Azra is in New York."

"Yeah, that's a good one. And I'm in Canada, right? I wish."

"Azra is in New York."

"What? What do you mean?"

"Azra," he repeated slowly, "is in…New York."

"Why would she be in New York? No, she can't be in New York. There's no way. She left New York; she wouldn't go back."

"Azra has been working in medical school."

"No, that's impossible. She studied nursing at NYU, she's not a doctor. I would know. I would have seen something."

"When was the last time you spoke with Azra?"

"When she left. Five years ago. She can't be in New York."

"Max. You're going to be fine," Demir said. "Here take this." Demir ripped off half of a napkin and took a sleek black ball point pen out of his blazer jacket. Next, he wrote down the name of a hospital. He kept his penmanship messy, strategically, of course, but I could have read the address from fifty feet away.

"Thank you," I said desperately. "I guess this is where we leave each other."

"This is where you go home. Be careful, you don't need to be here anymore. You shouldn't be here."

I got up and left. As I exited, I pushed my seat out with my hips. My anger got the best of me. I didn't look back; for all I cared, Demir could kick rocks.

I rushed to the elevator and clicked the lobby button over eight times, as if lighting up the little circle was going to change anything.

"C'mon, c'mon, c'mon," I yelled.

Men dressed in all black, most likely part of security, started to walk towards me; but, luckily for me, I hopped in, and the elevator door shut.

"I have to get out of here," I said out loud as my knees buckled and I fell to the ground. I grabbed the rail that hung across the wooden elevator backdrop, lifted myself up, and composed myself. I hailed a cab and gave quick instructions to take me back to my hotel. I buried my head between my legs and screamed in frustration. I had traveled all the way across the world for her. I had taken her (mentally) everywhere I had gone prior to that, and now I would leave without her only to find out that she was back in New York the whole time. The irony.

I walked into my hotel lobby like a wounded soldier. Yes, I could still carry myself home, but I would never be the same, knowing what I know now. I just wanted to go to sleep, but after a few drinks, it was only right that I go to the hotel bar. I think a part of me wanted one more conversation, just one more interaction, one more life lesson before I returned to the Big Apple.

The bartender was older than me but couldn't have been a day over forty. He had his sleeves rolled up with tattoos that lined his forearms all the way around the veins that pumped into his biceps. The pencil on his ear was mostly for show, but it still held utility as he lifted it off the crevasse that rested on his faded haircut. As he lifted his left arm up to adjust his sleeves, I saw a beautifully inked 'Brooklyn Bridge' that interlocked with the lower lying skyline of Istanbul.

"What can I get for you?" he asked.

"Are you from the city?"

"It's funny you ask," the man said, washing out a pint glass with a grey towel that had seen better days.

"I'm a big fan of asking questions these days, I hope I'm not prying. Also, do you have a Stella by any chance?"

"Stella it is. You're not prying," he said as he aggressively got into the small edges of the glass. "I was born here in Turkey then moved to Brooklyn where I was raised until I was thirteen. Moved back here as a teenager, but I still carry Brooklyn with me, so I got this tatted."

"I love it," I said as I downed a large gulp of my drink. "I love it, I love it," I repeated.

For me, it was hard to make conversation with men I didn't know. I wasn't shy, but I never related to the men who worked for a living. I was so used to my cubicle and my office life; it was my safe spot. In some ways, I felt guilty—I knew nothing about this man and what he had. For all I knew, he could have been a trust fund kid, working this job for fun, maybe to pick up women.

"And you?" he asked.

"Yes, I'm probably going to head back there early in the morning," I scrolled on my phone to pick a last-minute flight home.

"Well, it's not a bad place to go back to."

"No, not at all," I replied.

Then, as the conversation died down, a man, most likely in his mid to late sixties, sat down beside me. He lifted his hands up like he had been there before. I guess the usual meant something different to each individual guest.

"You don't look like you're from here, young man."

"That's because I'm not," I replied. "But not to worry, I'm leaving soon."

"Well, I hope you enjoyed your stay," the older man told me.

"I didn't," I said with a chip on my shoulder.

The bartender looked at me with suspicion as he continued to clean the depths of his pint glasses.

"We certainly can't please everyone. There's a billion something people in the world; everyone wants to be happy, everyone wants to be in love, everyone wants success."

"I just wanted to find my college girlfriend, okay? But I found out she's not in Turkey anymore. So, yeah, I'm leaving, and I'm not happy."

"What's your name, kid?"

"Max, yours?" I took another sip as the man leaned closer.

"Eymen."

"That's a cool name," I said. I was drunk and full of surprises, there was no filter in my cadence.

"It's a name."

"So, what other life advice do you have for me, Eymen?"

"What are you so worked up about, son?"

"Worked up?"

"You seem worked up," Eymen said

"Am I worked up?" I asked the bartender.

"A little bit," the bartender reassured Eymen. "But, in his defense, he's a New Yorker. Long trip, can you blame him?"

"Well, she missed out," Eymen said as he spun his glass around.

The glass—oh, was this small glass symbolic? It's elegance and grace. It was the little things about the glass, like the way the light shined through it. How subtle it sat in the palm of your hand, how gently it rested on a flat surface.

"She missed out; you don't even know her."

"Neither do you," Eymen said. His age was showing as wisdom bled from his lips.

"What's that supposed to mean?"

"You came here to Turkey only to find that your college girlfriend is no longer in Turkey. It sounds like you also do not know her."

I pounded my fist in anger against the wooden countertop. "Enough."

"Woah, sir, if you can't behave yourself, I'm going to call security," the bartender not so much threatened, but warned me.

"Okay, okay. I'll settle down."

"I was just trying to make you feel better, give you some words of comfort, friendly advice from an old sport like myself."

"No, you're right. Maybe I don't truly know her."

"Well, like I said. It's her loss."

"What do you mean by that?"

"Well, she lost out on a man that was willing to hop on a plane and go halfway across the globe to look for her. One day, she will come looking for you, but you won't be there for her."

I took another sip of my drink and attempted to process what the man had just told me. I looked at the bartender and he lifted his eyebrows in agreement with Eymen.

"The women who refuses to buy the clock for you now will sell their time for a premium. Don't you worry, my boy."

"So, how about you, then? Were you screwed over by some woman you once loved? What's your story?"

"Oh no, not me," Eymen said. "I was a lucky one."

"So, you're married?" I asked.

"Was married."

The bartender looked at me with disdain as he continued on with those glasses and his distressed towel.

"Oh, well, what happened?"

"She passed, yeah, she passed," Eymen said.

"I'm really sorry, I didn't mean to sound insensitive."

"We honeymooned in New York, actually. She always wanted to see the buildings. Something about that city... She wasn't from there, but I still remember when the plane approached the Big Apple, she shouted, 'I'm home.' Oh, wasn't that something!" Eymen reminisced.

The bartender smiled as he grabbed his drink and refilled it without question.

"It is something else, it truly is something else." I rubbed my eyes, signaling that I should be headed to bed.

"Welp, you either get to spend your life with the one you love, or you get stuck chasing the one who got away. Either way, sooner or later, you end up chasing. Heck, maybe it's better off chasing, that way you never know what you had. Good night, boys, and son, good luck with the girl. I have a feeling you will see her soon."

I tipped my bottle to Eymen as he exited the lobby bar.

"Looks like you know that man from somewhere?" I asked the bartender.

"He owns a few restaurants and hotels in the city. He's a rich man. It's kind of a routine for him to stop by. He means well, delivers wisdom; we like having him."

"I liked him," I said. "What a night."

I closed my tab and headed back to my room. I had booked a flight for seven hours out. It was around thirteen hundred dollars, but it was well worth the premium. As I got back into my room, I realized I could nap for about forty-five minutes, but not a minute more if I wanted to shower, double-check my carry-on, call a cab, and depart safely. I laid my eyes down but the pain I had from drinking resembled a hangover more than it did a buzz.

"Screw this," I screamed out.

I grabbed one of those really overpriced tall and heavy labeled water bottles, took it with me in the shower and sat down on the bench in the corner. I was so tired, from everything. But as I sat there—in the corner, naked—the water felt different this time around. It wasn't hot, it wasn't cold; it was perfect. I was forgiven from all the "what ifs" that circled around me. The guilt I placed on myself Azra suddenly leaving, the blame I stamped on my own neck. The self-doubt and insecurities I had about my career and the fear of underperforming suddenly went down the drain along with the body wash that cleansed my pores. I had never felt like my own man until that shower, if I'm being honest. When I was let go, I immediately thought it was me, that I must have said something sour or rubbed an intern the wrong way. But the reality was, I was good at this thing called life; I just had a few bad breaks. There I was, still standing. Still calling the shots.

I dried off and used the comb to part my hair just right. I put on a button-down oxford shirt, because how you dress says everything about you, even when you're leaving.

I walked to the elevator and made my way towards Sonya's room. I approached her door and lifted my arm to knock. I wanted to say goodbye, I wanted to thank her, I didn't want to depart without at least acknowledging the connection we had made. Yet, just as I was about to grip my knuckles together, I held back, stepping away from her door. Then, I wheeled my carry-on back to the elevator and departed to the lobby.

The front desk was professional as they extended their best wishes to me. It was around that same time that I put on my sunglasses. I started to channel my inner secret agent vibe, because after all, I was a man on a mission, but sadly, my current assignment was closed. I put my hand up for a cab and received a ride immediately. This time, the ride was quiet, eerie almost. But it didn't matter. I was on my way home. I was ready to confront the truth.

When I got to the airport, I realized what I had done and how insane it might sound five years from now, how crazy it may seem when I'm at a rooftop party in Brooklyn in my thirties. Nonetheless, this was my life.

When I got on the plane, I had no desire to do anything. I was done pretending to look productive by reading a book. I was through with motivational podcasts. I just wanted to go home, confront my past, and leave it behind me—leave it in the past.

"This is your pilot speaking. We are departing from Istanbul and will be arriving in Newark in approximately…" And that's all I remembered. I didn't dream, I didn't sit next to anyone fascinating, and I certainly didn't read a life-changing novel. I gave my body a break, and it was long overdue.

"Damn," I said under my breath as I woke up.

I let everyone filter out of the sky bus. I felt like the host of a New Year's Eve party as I waited behind, waving everyone goodbye with the hope that they would arrive home safely.

"Sir, sir, excuse me, sir," the flight attendant tried to get my attention.

"Oh, I'm sorry, I was just checking my phone."

"It's time to exit the plane."

"Of course, thank you."

I got off the plane and felt a feeling of emptiness as I walked through the terminal. There was no family to greet me, there was no girlfriend, no long-time friend who promised me a ride back home. There was just me and this new reality that I was learning to deal with. I had no job, yet ironically, money was not an issue, which I didn't know was a good thing or not. I was alone. But there was beauty in this realization. I concluded that I was never going to be able to completely understand why Azra chose to leave. I was never going to fathom why my boss, who had acted as my mentor, could lay me off like it was nothing.

But with all this struggle, I was happy, I was satisfied, I was content and in the craziest of circumstances, I re-found my confidence in the high school all-county soccer player who hadn't a worry in the world. I re-kindled my youth. I was alive.

I hopped in what had to be the third or fourth cab in a seventy-two-hour span. That's all I seemed to be doing these days. There was light rain, but I didn't mind because I could think better with the light drops on the windows.

"Where to?" This cab driver wasn't so friendly, yet there was a pleasant bedside manner to him.

I scuffled through my windbreaker and found the address that Azra's cousin had written down for me. It turned out to be the same address as the Weill Cornell Medical Center, which happened to be located a few hundred yards away from Colt's brownstone, where he lived with his wife and kids. I instructed the driver to take me to where Azra worked. It was about seventy minutes out if you considered the weather. For the next sixty minutes, my stomach was in a knot as I thought about the two people who had shaken up my life the most. The continuing theme of the last few months was Azra's glass. It summed up everything—our relationship, late nights in the city staying out drinking until 4 a.m. when the last call wasn't just a warning to go home but a sign to go to bed.

As we got closer to midtown, the final "thump" that the Uber made on the highway was enough to lift any tired man up straight. The skyline of New York City served as the last theme of nostalgia as I arrived home. The mist and fog that hung between the Chrysler building and some of the new construction gave me goosebumps. Once again, I was humbled by its monstrosity, looking down on me like an unruly child who ran away from home. I was greeted by its prowess but also grounded by its substance. The rain continued to hit the SUVs and trucks that zigzagged through the lanes, just like us, but more aggressive and urgent. I ran my fingers through my hair, swallowed my fears, and accepted the fact that I had to make my final statement before I would make peace with my fate.

"Get off here, please, kind sir," I ordered. My rhetoric typically was far less corny, yet at this stage in my life, or this era of my twenties, I channeled someone else, perhaps my father, or maybe even worse, my old boss, Colt.

"This good, young man?"

"Perfecto." I once again couldn't escape the ironic shades of who I was when I was nervous and the composure I wish I could maintain when I was scared.

And, so, just as my story started, it would end on foot. Or at least this chapter of my story. I had been to Colt's home before; it was gorgeous, almost too nice, too fancy for anyone who wanted to occasionally get their feet wet and experience the gritty side of New York. I had my carry-on dragging me back, but I wouldn't let it slow me down. I threw my knapsack over my shoulder and made my way to Colt's brownstone. I wasn't a real estate agent, except maybe on Zillow and Craigslist, but I knew a five-million-dollar estate when I saw one. How Colt managed to secure a listing as exquisite and well put together as his was more impressive than any business lecture I sat through.

I walked up to the front door that benefited from a naturally distressed look that younger buyers pay a lot of money for in the suburbs. I gave three knocks, and then, I waited patiently

Finally, someone answered the door. She was younger. She couldn't have been a week over twenty, and she chewed gum like a middle school student with an attitude problem.

"Who are you?" the girl asked.

"Who are *you*?" I smugly replied.

"You're on my property, plus I asked first," she wisely replied.

Her black sweatpants were rolled up and the white drawstring loosely hung under her silver belly button ring.

"Dad," she yelled as her left arm hung from the top left corner of the door. She swung with it like it was her favorite hobby.

"Perfect, that's who I wanted to see. By the way, what's your name?" I asked as I extended my hand.

"Nicole. So, how do you know my dad?"

"I worked for him."

There was an awkward pause.

"Oh, he was my boss."

"Stop," Nicole said.

"No, he was my boss."

"He never told me there was a cute boy at the firm."

"That's probably because he hates me. I mean, he fired me—he let me go, to be precise."

"Oh, I'm sorry, he can be a jerk sometimes."

"Honey..." Colt said in the background.

I poked my head inside as Nicole let her arms free from the door.

"You have a visitor, Dad."

"Ah, Max, what a surprise. I'll grab my coat."

132

Chapter 7: New York State of Mind
March 2020

Colt grabbed the first coat off the hook in the hallway that separated the staircase from the main living room. He gave Nicole a kiss on the forehead.

"Tell your mom I'm grabbing coffee with an old friend."

"Will do," she responded. She didn't want to be bothered, a typical college student.

"You have a nice daughter," I told Colt.

"Don't even go there."

"I wasn't implying anything."

Colt checked his cell phone quickly before he walked and talked with me. "I'm all yours. What's on your mind, kid?"

"Not too much. I was in the area, just wanted to catch up, thought maybe we could grab a coffee or something?"

"Sure, I know a spot just up the block," Colt assured me.

We made our way up the street and the shop held a neon light that appealed to Colt's generation, not so much mine, but I appreciated the character of the café.

I sat down like I owned the place and Colt immediately put his jacket over the seat like a retail designer dressing a store manikin. "How do you like your coffee these days?"

"Whatever you're having, make it two."

I looked out the window and two young children walked along the sidewalk as their middle school backpacks dragged them down. The boy and girl couldn't have looked any different. The boy was tall, for his age at least, African American, skinny, and the girl was tiny, red hair with freckles and about eight or nine inches shorter than the boy. Yet, these differences made up so much of the compatibility of New York. Immediately, I thought of Azra. It was like she was with me, and in many ways, her presence was felt even more so inside myself as time ticked on and the clock dragged any remaining memories apart.

"I added extra sugar. Wife says I shouldn't, but to heck with her."

"No worries, you work out still. Still swimming?"

Colt was a competitive swimmer. Well, not a competitive swimmer, but someone who could hop in the pool and hold his own with the city's most elite and successful. Yet, I knew Colt also had an affair with an old "swimming buddy" from the local YMCA. Colt went out of his way to swim at the public facility just because of her. And, as much respect as I had for Colt as a mentor, he had hurt me. I knew his weak spots and didn't feel guilty exploiting them. Before my trip to Istanbul, a comment of that nature would have been absurd to think of, but because I had a little bit of culture and adversity in me, I decided I would start playing chess; I had outgrown checkers.

"Oh, you know, I don't swim as much as I would like," Colt smirked.

Colt had a way of making light of an awful situation. His wife didn't trust him; yet he used this particular conversation to his advantage, to pretend things were fine. He figured a smile couldn't hurt either party.

"So, Max, why did you really come knocking?" Colt asked.

And even though the man had taken so much from me, I was reminded of the kind soul who gave a young kid a chance, a start in the Big Apple, and suddenly, any malice or negative vibrations left my mind.

"I went to Turkey," I said.

"You went to Turkey? Did you go to one of those virtual reality exhibitions in Union Square? I've been meaning to get to one of those."

"No, I went to Istanbul. I flew to Turkey."

"Well, why did you go there?"

"I had a girlfriend," I said as I sipped my coffee and investigated the city streets. I pictured a woman with a long black jacket to be Azra smoking a cigarette, waiting for me to finish my coffee. Yet, that in its nature was just another form of my coping tactics, as the lady turned around and I was brought back to reality.

"Like a long-distance girlfriend? Did you meet her on one of these dating apps. You know, my daughters are on those apps, and I have to tell you, I'm not the biggest fan, but I'm fascinated by the algorithms."

"Do you ever listen, Colt?"

Suddenly, just like that, I had his attention. He sat up straight, gripped the coffee a little tighter, and looked me in the eye.

"When I can," Colt told me, sternly and steadily.

"We met in college, we lived together, conquered the city together."

"So, what happened?"

"I don't know."

"What do you mean you don't know?" Colt relaxed and shrugged in his seat. "You don't know?" he repeated himself as my frustration grew.

"I know how and when she left, but I don't know why she left."

Colt could see the anxiety growing within me. "Hey, it's okay. Come here, it's okay."

"I don't know why everything I have turns to dust. Why'd you let me go, boss?" I said as tears ran down my cheeks. I buried my head in my hands as Colt came to the side of the sleek, traditional table.

"Get up, let's take a walk, come on, get up."

I followed Colt to the door. I didn't know where we were going, but I was glad the college students who were three pages deep into their senior theses didn't have to witness my erratic behavior.

"Now you want to protect me or something?" I wiped the moisture from below my eyes. I could hear my dad in my ear, "quit crying punk," because that's all I knew. Bury the emotion and dig through the storm.

"How old do you think I really am?" Colt asked.

"I don't know...thirty-nine, forty maybe? what does this have to do with anything?"

"Thirty-nine? I wish. Max, I have a college-aged daughter. I'm not thirty-nine."

"How old are you?"

"I'm forty-five, I'm almost twice your age."

"Okay, so?"

"Does anything about my age and my career stick out to you?"

"I'm not sure what you're asking, I'm sorry."

"I'll give you a hint: September 11."

"So, you were working during 9/11? I'm sorry, I guess I never thought of it like that, I mean, a lot of people were working on 9/11. It's a big city."

We crossed the street and Colt took a sip of his coffee.

"You know, I had this mentor when I was your age. His name was Tim. He was my big brother at Cantor Fitzgerald when I was a junior commodities trader. My title was just a romanticized way to describe my role as a glorious intern, yet Tim was awesome to learn from. He was about ten years my senior, and he looked out for me, for the most part. Sure, at times there was tough love, but that was to be expected at a company as large as Cantor."

"You worked at Cantor Fitzgerald?"

"Yep," Colt answered as we crossed the city streets slowly yet swiftly.

"Based in the World Trade Center, Cantor Fitzgerald?"

"I started in late June, and after the fourth of July, every morning at 8:30, Tim would

137

make me run and get him coffee. It was sort of like a rite of passage."

"Jesus." The suspense of the story started to captivate my body.

"I'll never forget that morning, Tim was in such a good mood; he had been selected for a promotion."

"So that morning, on September 11, you went to get coffee."

"Yeah, he wasn't going to send me, but I was in a bad mood that morning—I had gotten into an argument with my girlfriend and Tim could sense it."

"So, what did he do?"

"Tim never hesitated, that's what made him a valuable associate for the firm. He reached into his wallet and handed me a ten dollar bill. It was sort of unspoken that the junior associate treated their mentors, but that morning, he paid my way."

"So, that coffee saved your life?"

"The coffee came out to nine dollars, I guess I was in a rush, not too concerned with the extra dollar, if anything, it was the tip for the cute barista."

"So, this was at 8:30, right? Weren't you in a position for disaster as you approached the office?"

"I thought I was, but you have to remember, this was 2001, and to some people, a dollar held more value than to others. So, as I was walking back to the office, the barista ran out to return the dollar to me."

"She walked all that way?"

"Well, it's the city, nothing's that far, maybe fifty yards."

"Go on." I waved Colt to continue as we navigated the city streets as masked New Yorkers stared on like we were crazy.

"I thanked her. She was beautiful. She was out of breath, but I think she was just nervous. She was finishing up her English degree, we got to talking, and I told her I had a girlfriend, but she was persistent."

"Do you remember her name?"

"Of course. Maria; she's my wife."

"She's your wife!" I yelled.

"Relax, Max, the story gets even crazier."

"Please, please, continue."

"Back in those days, we didn't have Instagram or Twitter, so I agreed to take her out and she took a pen out of her back pocket and gave me her address, then, we agreed on a date and time."

"But it was also September 11?" I had so many questions, and even though we were walking, I felt like I was on the edge of my seat at my hometown cinemas.

"It was around 8:45, so I had to get back to the office, and just like that, a bang about as loud as your tiny brain could imagine woke up the entire city of New York."

"The North tower was hit?"

"Yes, and I immediately grabbed Maria and bolted. The way the ground was shaking was enough to make a man run for it, but I had someone else to watch over now. Maria wanted to go back to the coffee shop; her things were in the café."

"Even in a time like that, who is crazy enough to think about work?"

"You see, my wife is a novelist, an author. Her first book was on the top shelf, right over the register. It was the only thing she cared about for years before we met."

"So, what happened next?"

"Well, I was quick on my feet back then. I grabbed her arm, but it was met with some resistance. I could hear her say, 'wait, wait, you don't understand, wait!' as we navigated our way through the Financial District.

"You didn't know at the time?"

"I didn't know." Colt shook his head.

"Hey, it's not your fault," I reassured him. "I mean, how were you supposed to know?"

Colt smiled in approval. "Yeah, I suppose you're right. Thanks, Max."

"But how did you leave the city? I mean, it had to have been mayhem, right?"

"I had been swimming a lot and working out, and my adrenaline was obviously at an all-time high," Colt explained. "So, I picked her up and sprinted towards the nearest curve in the street, hoping to find someone who hadn't seen what had happened up close. Keep in mind, not everyone knew what happened, or what was going to happen."

"Who did you find? What was the sentiment? Were people screaming?"

"It was chaos, uh, confusion, it was a state of disarray would be the most efficient way to describe things. There was a cab driver who was sleeping in his car, and he had woken up right when we got to the corner. The impact must have made its way to the vehicle as soon as we pulled up—that's how fast I was sprinting with Maria in my arms.

"I said, 'Sir, just drive, take us off the island, anywhere, anywhere, I will pay you anything, please let us get in, there's something going on, I don't know what it is, but it's not good,'" Colt explained as he collected the thoughts of a tragedy he never wanted to confront again; yet, here he was, reliving an almost unimaginable sequence of events.

"You didn't waste any time."

"There wasn't any time to waste," Colt said as he lectured me. We stopped walking and he looked me in the eye. "No time to waste, remember that."

"So, you really survived 9/11? I never knew that." I looked up. "I'm sorry I never knew that. What did you do once you found a cab? You went back home?"

"We drove into Brooklyn, then through Queens, then up to Greenwich, Connecticut. Most people meet their future wife's parents on a crisp summer day with family and friends by the pool. I met them on the morning of one of the worst attacks in US history."

"Rough, but it sounds like it worked out."

"I still remember having a drink with my father-in-law that same night. It was almost as if my future was destined for me. It was like I couldn't *not* marry this girl. We had already been

141

through a half century of turmoil, and we had only known each other for a few hours."

"What did your father-in-law say?"

"Well, obviously, it was a mid-September night, and the mood was set in Connecticut. The eerie part was you could see the smoke from the backyard; we were so close to ground zero yet light years away."

"He must have been happy you were there. You looked out for his daughter...I mean, he must have saw the world in you."

"Yeah, he offered me a job. He had a firm back home in Greenwich. Small boutique thing."

"Just like yours now?" I asked.

"Just like mine. Obviously, Cantor-Fitzgerald was a mess, and I was just a glorified intern. I would have been crazy to turn it down, especially if you heard the starting salary. I guess at the time it was a form of reparation for what I did for his daughter."

"It sounds like it was destiny, like it was meant to be. It was your big break."

"It was. But you know what the crazy thing was?"

"What?"

"I never processed Tim's death, or at least that day I didn't. It was like that cup of coffee gave me the world and it gave Tim absolutely nothing at all."

"But you got lucky. You did nothing wrong. It was a tragedy; Tim's death has nothing to do with you."

"I know, yet that day, his life was ending and mine was just beginning. Because I was at my boss's house every day, I was able to date my current wife. Tim gave me a clean slate, a fair chance, by handing me ten dollars for a coffee."

"The coffee saved your life."

"Now, listen, I know you probably hate me, and you think I'm an asshole, but me letting you go wasn't an insult; it was a clean slate, a second chance

I stuck my hand out and looked Colt in the eye. "Friends?" I asked.

Colt pushed my hand away and came in to hug me. "Family," he said as he brought me in. "Now, go do what you have to do."

So, with that, I understood what I had to accomplish next.

Colt checked his watch. "I better get going," he added.

And just like that, we were on our way, not just for the moment, but maybe forever.

"Me too, Colt. Thanks for the coffee."

"Of course."

Chapter 8: Stories of the Past
March 2020

      The Upper East Side was filled with shops, restaurants, street vendors, and hospitals. I had the address crumpled up on a small piece of paper, but for the most part, I knew where I was going from memory. I unwrapped the piece of paper that read: *Weill Cornell Medical Center.* There was no mystery; I had walked by these facilities, tens or maybe even hundreds of times throughout my tenure of NYC living. So, this was it—time to confront my past, and, most importantly, time to start embracing my future.

      "How the hell did I get here?" I said out loud as a cab almost swiped half my upper torso.

      "Jesus Christ. Watch where you're going!" I saw a middle finger sticking out of the driver's side window. To think that Azra was potentially working across the street frightened me at first; however, after the humbling conversation with Colt, I began to feel at ease and even ready to confront the harshest of my realities. I used the street vendor as a body shield just in case Azra had walked outside for a cigarette (although the thought of her holding onto such an immature habit was disturbing, to say the least).

      "Hello, sir, sorry to bother you, but do you have any facemasks available?"

      "How many you need?" The middle-aged man had his sleeve rolled up, eager to sell masks while his face courageously showed the opposite of any kind of fear towards this coronavirus that was conquering victims hour by hour. The irony was riveting.

"Can I grab a few?"

"I do five for ten dollars. Deal?"

"Ten dollars? For masks?"

"Very hard to find right now, very hard to find. This is good deal."

I took a crisp, folded, and pleasant smelling ten dollar bill and slapped it down on the silver-plated counter that divided me from the man as the hot dogs and pretzels sizzled in the background.

"Stay safe," he said as I quickly ripped the plastic bag in two and three or four masks emptied into my hands.

I quickly put one on and adjusted it around my chin. I enjoyed the disguise but despised the discomfort. I stared at the hospital entrance as security directed four or five stretchers holding patients with oxygen masks firmed tightly to their mouths.

"Armageddon," a man my age said as he waited for my response.

I handed him an extra mask; it was the least I could do. "Looks like you may need one of these," I told him.

"Thank you, I'll throw this on when I hop on the Q train. Stay safe, and get ready for the end of the world," the man said as he backpedaled toward the subway entrance.

Then, as I walked even closer to the hospital facility, I was alarmed by the cries and shouts of two female physicians as they buried their heads in their hands. It was at this moment; I

145

could see the severity of the situation surrounding the coronavirus. I walked closer to the two women, yet I was still far from where they sat. I grabbed my phone and touched the home screen to blend into the crowd and protect my anonymity. I kept my mask tight and secure. My chin itched as did my nose, but it was a small price to pay for going undercover in a city where every individual was exposed to the elements of not just chemicals and bacteria but also acquaintances and friends. The young physician, her stethoscope hanging over her neck like a necklace, began to adjust her mask. She lowered it enough that I could make out her face.

"Azra?" I said out loud.

Knots began to form in my stomach as well as a lump in my throat. I took a deep breath but was almost brought to my knees as I clenched onto side of an MTA bus stop. If seeing her wasn't tough enough, having to deal with the acquaintance that followed almost put me over the edge. As Azra collected herself, a man, no taller than 6'5" but not shorter than 6'1", approached her. At first, Azra resisted, then, as the man with the NYU Law School crew neck came forward, Azra moved back once more. I moved and ducked behind the NYC water sewer, but because I was adjusting my height, I drew more attention to my stature.

"Yusef. I knew it," I said under my breath. My own confirmation wasn't enough; I had to say it out loud. My isolation started to attract others as pedestrians walking on the street looked at me in pity. Still, I continued to hide, even though the reality was slowly but surely setting in. I walked back to the street vendor.

"I'm not particularly hungry, but I need you to help hide me for just a second. While I'm waiting, here's ten bucks. I guess I'll take a hot dog with ketchup, and screw it—a Pepsi, why not." And just like that, my story came full circle, with a hot dog and a Pepsi, just how it started. The vendor took his time and re-adjusted the radio as warnings of the coronavirus began to circulate even further.

"You hear this shit?"

"Yeah, getting bad, huh? Why do you think I bought these face coverings?" I told the vendor as I adjusted my mask.

Eventually, the vendor handed me the hot dog with two beige-colored napkins wrapped around the Pepsi that functioned as both a hand warmer and a coaster.

"We stay open though. The city doesn't sleep."

I re-directed my vision toward Azra. Maybe I was overthinking the scenario, maybe Azra didn't leave the thread on Twitter for me to see. I never thought that at my age I would be worried about Twitter drama, yet, here I was, fighting my past while trying my best to live in the moment. My negative feelings began to shift as the sentiment drifted towards the positive. It was really Azra.

After all this time and all the countless memories we shared, she was back. I suddenly became happy, almost like I accomplished a lifelong milestone. I was validated. But then, the man came closer, and he grabbed her by her waist. Azra graciously removed her mask. The man's hands went up towards her chin and then to her forehead as he gently kissed her just below her temple. He lowered his lips, so they met hers, and that's when my past and my present truly met.

I thought about the slide tackle when I first met Azra. The first time we made love. The smile of hers when she shook the keys to our first apartment. I thought about our first date, even the first fights we had. It was never just the highs that made our relationship worth reminiscing—it was also the lows.

I threw the Pepsi in the trash and wiped the grease and ketchup off my lips with the napkin that was now soaked with moisture. I saw the man hug her goodbye, so I followed. I had already foolishly flown to Turkey, what was one more trip in my own city? As the man walked away, I began to trail him. I followed and followed until I was brought to the Q train. I made sure my mask was secure. If it slipped, he would have more than likely recognized me from somewhere, I mean, who doesn't discuss prior relationships, especially if you lived with that person?

I stayed ten paces behind the man, who, for the moment, we will refer to as "law student," (even though I knew it was probably Yusef), his NYU crew neck sticking out like a sore thumb as the downtown express train approached. The train was crowded but not overwhelmingly congested as I grabbed the pole and used it to navigate my way to an open seat. Half the passengers were wearing a face mask while the other half rolled the dice and played Russian Roulette with a virus that we knew little to nothing about.

"Stand clear of the closing doors, please. Bing-Bong."

The noise of the automated conductor was a reminder that as much as the city changed, some things would always remain the same. I tried to position myself close to the law student while also looking ahead, trying to play it cool. His posture was relaxed yet not too nonchalant. His back arched while his penny loafers lightly tapped as they lifted a quarter of an inch on the black rubber generic subway flooring. His head melodically bopped in sequence to the subtle bumps and vibrations that the train car took through its duration. He then opened a rugged, distressed, yet relevant novel, "The Firm," by John Grisham. It was cliché, and if it had been late October, I might have mistaken his pose for a Halloween costume.

"Bing-Bong. Stand Clear of the closing doors, please."

We continued our way downtown. I had to go this way to get home, so for me, I was killing two birds with one big stone. The law student brought the book closer to his view, slowly turning the pages. There could have been a mugging taking place in front of his eyes, but the idea of checks and balances in the justice system only seemed to make sense in the vanilla crème pages of his fiction novel. But, just like myself, most residents of New York City weren't originally from here, and they still had a lot to learn when it came to street smarts.

"This is a Coney Island bound Q train. The next station is 14th street (Union Square). Stand Clear of the closing doors, please."

Immediately, the law student slammed his book, a student ID pass or perhaps a library card serving as a placeholder. A man with a curriculum as competitive and tradition as strong as NYU shouldn't have time for recreational reading, but this was the New York City subway system—an underground time warp. The doors opened again, and, at first, the law student stayed put, but then, he collected himself and walked out as his leather bag hung across his right shoulder. I clicked my phone, pretended to be lost, and slowly exited the machine.

The law student walked fast and with confidence as his leather bag—which better suited an author more than it suited an aspiring juris doctor—dangled from his side. The law student was tall, dark, and with even darker hair. This was in fact Yusef. He fit every description, and it was obvious that Azra had a history with this man that went back further than just Twitter direct messages. I realized I could not follow him forever; I soon had to come to terms with the truth and the reality of how hard this awakening would hit. Eventually, after so many steps in the direction of the East Village towards the neighborhood of Astor Place, the law student slowed down. For whatever reason, he had been holding his novel in his right hand with his cell phone in his back pocket. Maybe holding the novel kept him closer to the story, or maybe it just felt like New York City to him. He ended up at a luxury building that was mixed in with a bunch of college dorms and academic-funded housing.

"Son of a bitch," I said under my breath.

"Greetings, Yusef," the doorman said from six feet away.

Everyone was taking precautions, there was no need to shake hands. But, from that, I had confirmation: it was Yusef.

"Thank you, Harold," Yusef said.

Harold, what a typical name for a doorman, I thought to myself.

"Azra will be late tonight; they need all the staff they can get, even the residents."

I was confused by what Yusef, the man formerly known as the law student, said to his doorman. And then, just like that, it clicked. It began to finally make sense. Azra was not a nurse, she was a medical doctor. This fact for me was soul crushing, Azra didn't need me to succeed. She didn't want to share a shoebox apartment with me in New York to simply live and get by.

Azra had moved on. I wasn't even an afterthought, let alone an existing memory in her mind, or vague dream in her sleeping hours. I was making a fool of myself and found it best to hop back on the subway, go home, and face the hard truth—I was done chasing Azra, for good.

That subway ride felt different. Often, this city was a place of hope and endless possibilities, but now, I was left broken, still with many unanswered questions. I felt like a tourist in my own home. But the good news was that out of all the experiences, places, and feelings that Azra had put me through, I was still here. I was still taking the subway home; I was still learning, growing, and adjusting.

Suddenly, a homeless man started to sing. Maybe he had grown up around the same era as Frank Sinatra, until I started to crunch the math and realized the rat pack would have been thirty years older than this poor old soul. Still, music was music, and it didn't matter where it was coming from, as long as I could sing along and find a silver lining, and that's exactly what I did. So, I got of the train and called my dad, and he quickly texted me that he was busy. Of course, typical employed lawyer talk. Busy man with responsibilities. So, I texted him back.

"Dad, when you can, tell Mom to throw out the old letters from Azra. Thanks, love you both. Talk soon."

My phone vibrated again. It was Megan. Even though my soul was crushed, I still looked forward to the prospect of seeing Megan. It was part revenge and part comfort. I actually liked her, and, most importantly, it was clear she always liked me.

"Can I stop by? I'm in the area." Megan asked with a wink face.

Megan was ferocious. This bothered me to think about, even if it was by myself and to myself, the thoughts seemed immature and immoral. But now, Azra was with her new man, in the same city that I helped her conquer, helped her establish herself in. She had started a new chapter. But if New York was a novel, that means every character can be in love in one chapter, and enemies in the next.

"Come over," I demanded. "Come over now, we have a lot to talk about."

I prepared my apartment and showed in hopes that I could metaphorically wash Azra away, one last time. I learned if you wanted to clean up fast, all you had to do was put things back in right angles. But, before I could put things back where they belonged, Megan was at my door.

Ding-Dong

My doorbell was way more intense than it had to be given the square footage. Megan let herself in.

"I have such great news."

She had a bottle of wine in a pouch bag, it was as if the bag was made strictly for wine, and I didn't hate it.

"Sure, take a seat. What's up?" I asked. "Everything okay?"

"More than okay," Megan said. "It's actually amazing! Here, grab a glass. I really want to celebrate."

I took two tall glasses out of the top cabinet. They weren't handcrafted for wine; if anything, they would have worked for a Pilsner, but they did the trick. "What are we celebrating?"

"Okay, you ready?"

"Yes, tell me, tell me," I said as the wine hit the topsides of the glasses like snow falling down the mountains in an avalanche.

"I got accepted to a three-month showcase in Hollywood. I leave in May."

"Wait, Megan! This is absolutely incredible. No wonder you've been so nervous lately; it makes sense now. I'm so proud of you."

"I knew you would be happy for me. How was your trip, if it's okay that I ask?"

"I'm home now, it's done, that's all you need to know."

"Okay, anyway, what do you think?"

"You said you leave in May?" I questioned. "Why are your bags here?"

"Well, okay, so that's what I wanted to ask you…"

I readjusted myself on the couch. "Ask me what?"

"Well, just because with everything going on, would it be okay if I stayed here

154

at least until April, and then I can be out, and I can find a cheap hotel and do an extended stay."

I took a step towards Megan and cupped her chin into the palm of my hands. "Don't be silly," I reassured her. "Of course, you can stay here. Plus, I could use the company. I don't know if you've been keeping up with the news, but you may want to board that flight sooner rather than later."

"Is it that bad?" Megan asked.

"It's not good. I'm nervous about what it could do to the city."

"I mean, Max, it's New York City. Don't worry, it's not going anywhere."

"I hope you're right."

"Well, anyway, there are a few more things I have to clear out of my old place. Do you mind if I head back here later tonight? Just need to scoop a few items and I'll be back before midnight. Deal?"

Megan had a way of talking like an established housewife at a garage sale on Long Island. She was always pleasantly negotiating something, even though her aura was so innocent and pure.

"That's perfect, works for me, roomie."

"Just temporary roomie, don't get ahead of yourself."

"You're the one staying here, Megan."

"I appreciate it very much." Megan gave me a kiss as she left the apartment.

I stared down at Megan's bags. I felt extremely apathetic, confused, and unsettled. I grabbed an old lifeguard bathing suit from my high school days. The pool that set comfortably and luxuriously on my rooftop often went unused, and there were almost never any swimmers in the four lanes. In fact, the only guest was the seventeen-year-old lifeguard who probably lived on the Upper East Side, who had one headphone in, one headphone out. I threw a towel on my shoulder and made my way to the elevator and towards the rooftop. I threw the towel on an old beaten and distressed lounge chair. I gave a head nod to the lifeguard; his calculator and graph paper out on the table next to him. I could still envision those long nights of studying. I took a dive in and forgot my thoughts, just for a moment.

Sleeping after a good swim was an excellent way to put your mind at ease. It reminded me of the way I used to sleep after a family vacation. The chlorine encouraged me to take a cold shower and head to bed. I was exhausted, and I wondered why I wasn't swimming more often. I decided to brush my teeth after a quick shower, the towel wrapped around my hips and the faucet lightly gracing a new brush that I picked up from the local CVS. Life was funny; we spent all day in our bodies but rarely really see ourselves. The only time of the day where I saw what I looked like was when I brushed my teeth. I noticed pimples that I didn't know existed (probably from stress). I saw bags under my eyes from sleepless nights and unnecessary early mornings, but ultimately, I saw myself. I saw me for who I was, what I went through, and what I had yet to experience. I looked at the newly formed abs that started to appear and the veins that stuck out in my shoulders. I admired the progress; I hadn't had a definition like this since I was a freshman at NYU, and most of the time, it only took twenty pushups a night, go figure. As I extended my shoulders and flexed my biceps, the doorbell rang. My doorman called my apartment phone simultaneously, which was fixed into the wall like a fire switch in an elementary school.

"Visitor," the front desk attendant said.

"Yep, got it," I responded.

The phone call was merely a "heads up" more than anything else, but it was still a nice luxury, nonetheless.

What I saw next was a complete stranger yet a familiar face, all at the same time. I assumed it was Megan, so I didn't think to throw a shirt on. Instead, I flirted before I saw her face. "Oh, so you're back for more huh? Couldn't let me—" And then I was cut off.

"Azra?" I said as my heart skipped a beat. My face turned red. She looked the same as when I first laid my eyes on her. All of my memories were instantly more vivid, like a yearbook of photos that were saved from the fire and returned back to the owner.

"Come in." I went forward to give Azra a hug while simultaneously grabbing a shirt from the counter next to the wall.

"Max, I work at a hospital. I think it's better if we keep our distance. You look good though, if that makes you feel better," Azra said as her eyes wandered toward the bags that sat on the living room floor. Her eyes quickly directed back to me like she saw nothing.

"Okay, fair enough," I said.

I went to pour Azra a glass of water, I didn't ask this time. If she came here unannounced after abruptly leaving, then, well, the least she could do was accept my water.

I walked over to her. "Here, just take this."

"I don't want water," Azra said. "But thank you."

"Wine?" I asked. Her head nod was subtle but significant, "Yes, please, hurry." Just like that, I was back to working as Azra's personal assistant.

I didn't know what to say as my hand shook and my elbow twitched. "Red or white?"

Azra looked at me again. She didn't say anything, but her eyes told me everything. "Are you serious?" It was always white wine with Azra, the opposite of Megan.

"So," I said. "You're a doctor?"

I poured a heavy glass. There was only one clean wine glass, and I stared at the decade-old crystal whiskey glass that laid next to me the same night Azra left. The way it sat on the shelf made my mind rewind to that night, to those moments of fear and anxiety that shortly followed.

"How do you know?" Azra said as she accepted the glass.

I rested my back in an upright position against the couch.

"What do you mean?" I asked. I played dumb. As much as I was onto Azra, she was onto me.

"Yusef, I guess he recognized you."

"Yusef?" I asked.

"Max, please. I know you know. I know everything."

"Okay, well, what do you know?"

"You're crazy," Azra said. "But you care, and I admire you for that."

I looked down. I couldn't decide if I was ashamed or scared of saying the wrong things. "Why did you come here?"

"To tell you what happened?"

We both laughed. We were further than six feet apart, but it felt as if our hearts were inches away.

"I'm listening. But wait, you know, I finally went to Europe, Istanbul, to find you, just to find out that you were here. It is indeed a small world after all.

"I know, my cousin told me. He liked you very much. I can't believe you went there, all those years I begged you to come when we were in college."

"We both know I wasn't allowed to come. That was your escape, always was and always has been," I said.

159

"You still know me too well, don't you, Max?"

We laughed again, and the years of bitterness and resentment began to fade. I was naturally healed by the time that passed. There she was—beautiful, established, so many memories away from who we used to be. So many holidays, birthdays, and times apart. There were unfortunate deaths in our families, where we both lacked each other to cry on, summer nights at the beach spent somber and alone in a blanket staring at the stars wishing for her. Soon, those thoughts overtook the happiness I had felt upon her arrival, and anger enraged me. I contained myself, though. After all these years, I had learned to harness the gun and settle the violence.

"Well, at least now I can say I've been to Europe and Asia. Not bad for a finance bro who was too afraid to leave the country."

"You're still funny, I see," Azra sipped her wine and clenched her glass tightly. She scanned the living room at Megan's luggage, but once again, failed to say anything.

"Some may say," I looked down at my glass. I shook it in hopes that it would stir my creativity in a time where I so desperately needed it the most.

"Look, I just wanted to explain a few things," Azra said.

I rolled my eyes. I laughed. But it wasn't one of those 'friendly, it's okay we are *cool,*' eye rolls. It was packed with years of resentment. But, like my mother always reminded me, I was a lover, not a fighter, and I gave her the floor.

"Go on," I told her.

"You know I never wanted to leave, all those years back, I love it here in New York."

"No, I did not know that."

"Let me finish, please."

Azra had a way of slowing me down while controlling the momentum. It was maybe her greatest strength, or quite possibly, my biggest weakness.

"You have a right to explain yourself, I suppose."

"When I left that early morning, it was for a reason."

"I'm listening."

"When I was a senior in high school, my friend Derya and I took a trip late at night."

"What kind of trip?"

"Just a drive. Derya had gotten into a fight with her parents. They were always fighting with each other; Derya's parents didn't understand her."

"So, you went with Derya?"

"At first, I said no, I should have just gone back to bed. But she kept calling, and she was like a sister to me. I couldn't ignore her calls; she could have been in danger."

"Where did you go?"

"At first, it was a normal drive, just to get away and let out some steam, you know, typical high school behavior."

"Yes, I think we've all been there."

"So, of course, I snuck out while my parents were sleeping, but I didn't feel guilty, because she was like a sister to me. I had to go."

The way that Azra said 'she was,' in the past tense frightened me. I swallowed my saliva and arched my back once more. I was in for a story that I was not prepared to hear.

"So, what happened?"

"At first, Derya started to drive fast, but she did not have a license. It frightened me. What started as an adventure quickly turned into a nightmare. Then she told me where we were going only after I screamed at her and demanded an answer."

"Where was she taking you?"

"She told me we were going to a club…to drink, smoke, and lose our virginities."

The plot in the story turned grey. Suddenly, it was all making sense. The different cultures and how they so elegantly clashed. Turkey and America, both nations with established cities, militaries and authority, but so entirely different, not just when it came to ethics and code but also in terms of religion and value.

"You did the right thing, it sounds like you resisted. You were not ready for that? I would not have been ready for that."

"Max, it was so late. It was dark and I was so scared, Max. I was so scared. I was terrified, I am still terrified of how easily I got into her car, and how easily I left with her only to be destined for a trip that I simply did not want to take."

Azra's eyes started to tear up.

"It's okay, keep going, I'm here, I'm listening."

"I just wanted to go home, and I begged her to take me back, but Derya's family, it's complicated. It wasn't that easy to get her to follow my commands."

"What happened next? Azra, it's okay, I'm here, I can listen."

"I had no choice but to grab the wheel. I wasn't trying to steal control from her. I was just trying to show her that I didn't want to be there anymore. We lost control of the car and crashed into the side roadblock."

"Azra," I whispered. I didn't want to interrupt her; I had to let her continue.

"I was fine, Max. I was fine. You know? I had a couple of scratches on me. I thought Derya was fine, too. I just assumed if I was fine, that she was fine. But she was bleeding from her forehead. She wasn't responding. I was so scared, Max."

"It was not your fault, you were just trying to do the right thing, Azra, it's so important that you know that."

"I know that now, but I called for police and an ambulance. Derya was immediately put into an induced coma. I have to live with that, Max, okay?"

"Is that why you left that night? Is that why you had to take off almost without notice?"

"The night I left, Max, Derya was taken off life support. I was going home to say goodbye."

I stared at Azra in shock. It was a moment I will never forget. To see someone's pain and know you could never do anything about it. To have feelings for someone, meanwhile, her college roommate's luggage is in your apartment. Azra knows, she definitely knows.

"Had I known, Azra, it would have changed everything. Why couldn't you tell me?"

"Because throughout our relationship, I had grown close to Derya's brother. It was like the only thing we had was each other through Derya. I'm so sorry, Max." Azra began to break down in tears.

I crawled over to Azra and held her while she yelled. These were not cries or tears or emotional releases, these were moans of anger and frustration.

"I'm so sorry, Max. I love you. I love you, and I miss you."

"I love you, too. It's okay Azra."

"And I'm sorry that I never took you home. You were the best boyfriend."

"I still love you, always, Azra. It's okay. Now I understand. I find myself at peace now. Thank you for sharing this with me. I'm so sorry, I love you, Azra."

"You were and you are the greatest thing to ever happen to me. But I had to go home for some time, to battle my demons head-on."

"It's okay."

I kissed Azra on the forehead.

"But now, Azra, we can talk about this. You and Yusef are back? Why are you back?"

Azra collected her tears and tried to catch her breath, but with every deep inhale in hopes of collecting her thoughts, she was set back a few seconds. "NYU allowed me to finish classes via online curriculum for nursing. After visiting Derya at the hospital, I knew there was more out there for me. So, I applied for medical school in Istanbul. I was accepted. I was almost set to graduate when they recommended an early waiver to come to the United States to fight the coronavirus. It was always Yusef's dream to go to law school, and his grades were sufficient for NYU."

"I am so proud of you, and Yusef sounds great."

"He is, and I know this is difficult to hear, but he reminds me of you in the most beautiful way. He knows everything about you. I talk to him about you all the time."

"That is nice to hear. So, you're staying here in New York?"

"Yes, Max, for now, I don't know how long this coronavirus will be going on for, but it's bad. It's very bad. I need you to stay safe."

I started to let go of Azra and retreat. I didn't want to get too close.

"Azra," I said.

"Yes, Max?"

"I don't want to sound like a jerk, but I also need you to know something."

"Yes, what is it?"

"One day, there's a chance that you may need me, for whatever reason, but just know that even though I said I would always be there for you, there's a good chance that I won't be able to be there for you."

"What does that even mean?"

The mood shifted immediately. "I can't just be someone you lean on. I meant more to you than that, I have to respect myself."

"I just poured my heart out to you. What are you saying?"

"I am so sorry for what happened to you before college and during our relationship. But I'm even more sorry that you could never share any of it with me."

"I wanted to share it with you, it was complicated."

"And I respect that. But I waited for you. I held on to the idea of us. I just got laid off, and one of the first things I did was go to Istanbul, and you can find it weird and strange, but I did not go there looking for you."

"Then why did you go?"

"I was looking to see the world that influenced you before you met me."

"Did you find it?"

"No, honestly, I didn't. I wanted to think that culture, religion, family, and social norms were so different there, but everything was exactly the same."

"I'm sorry you didn't find what you were looking for."

"No, I think I did, I found out that we were both just people, and it didn't matter where we came from. We both shared something unique."

"And what is that?"

"We loved each other."

"Max, can I ask you another question?"

"Yes."

"I recognize those bags in the living room. Are you seeing her?"

"What are you asking, Azra?"

"Megan. Are you sleeping with her?"

I looked down. Never in my wildest dreams would I have thought I would be confronting a scenario as sensitive as this one.

"Azra," I replied without a backup plan for what she would ask next.

"Just look up if it's true."

Azra and I stared at each other for about seven or eight seconds, but it felt like ten lifetimes. We both knew I would look up, but the question was when? Every second I held out was another eternity of pain, yet, for some reason, I continued the torture. Then, after about fourteen or fifteen seconds, I lifted my head to look at the ceiling. I quickly looked back down, ashamed and scared. I was terrified of my fate, absolutely sick to my stomach. Azra shook her head as tears rushed down her cheeks and funneled through the veins of her neck, almost like the human anatomy was designed just for this moment.

"I should have never introduced you to Megan," Azra said as she flailed her arms. "Megan was my first friend. She was *my* friend."

"I don't know what to say, Azra. I don't know what to say."

"There's nothing left to say. I lost my first two friends here."

"Come, here," I said as I begged for Azra's warmth, even for one last time.

"No, do not touch me."

I became desperate, but I didn't want to be too rough on myself. I remembered the early morning when she left like it was yesterday, there was no sense of reason or respect. As much as Azra had a right to be mad, well, so did I. I didn't want to forget that, ever.

"Maybe I should leave."

"Hey, do you love him?"

Azra looked back at me. "Does it matter?"

"I guess not."

Azra shook her head and exited the apartment. "I would have never done that to you."

I sat back down against the couch.

"I messed up." I got up and walked to the elevator in hopes of tracking Azra down. She already had to be on the main floor by now. I was toast. I tapped the orange elevator "down" button over ten times.

"C'mon, c'mon, c'mon." I yelled.

Eventually, it came, and I made my way down to the lobby. I got to the very bottom and walked outside to the city street. I looked to the left, then scanned to the right. A cab drove by, and that was it. Maybe it carried Azra, maybe she was walking the city streets looking for a dimly lit tavern where she could down a shot to forget about life itself, or maybe she was on the subway, with lonely people like herself in hopes of company. As for me, I walked back up to my unit, went to bed, and sat on my phone until Megan got back. I felt like a student who had after-school detention and was waiting for my mom to leave work so she could take me home.

Eventually, Megan knocked on the door. I went to let her in as my stomach formed imaginary circles around a perfectly tied knot.

"Hey, I'm back, I'm exhausted! Did you eat?"

"Yeah, I'm fine," I lied. I couldn't put anything into my stomach. "Want to come to bed, lay down together?"

"But it's only ten o'clock?" Megan replied. She was confused but not upset.

"Yeah, we can watch a movie?"

"That sounds perfect. Do you have microwaveable popcorn by any chance?"

"Yeah!"

Megan caught me by surprise. I hadn't eaten the popcorn in bed since I was in middle school, but I suppose now my living space was overtaken.

Megan put on a rom-com, and it didn't make it any better. 'Definitely Maybe', a movie starring Ryan Reynolds. It was about a young man who moved from the Midwest to NYC to work on an election. Throughout the whole film, I showed disinterest, like I was mad or frustrated, which I was.

"Are you upset, Max?"

"No, I'm not upset. It's just that…I have to tell you something." I put my phone on the nightstand.

"Oh, okay, is it something I did?"

"No, that's not it. Azra came over when you were gone earlier."

Megan's jaw dropped. "Azra was here?"

"Yes."

Megan crawled across the bed as the sheets got tangled in our legs and knees. She gave me a kiss. "Are you okay?"

"Yes, you're not mad?"

"I'm not mad."

"You knew?"

"Most of it," Megan said. "I think most of it. I don't want to know anymore. I want to forget about her, for now, if that's cool?"

"Megan?"

"Yes, Max."

"I'm always going to miss her."

"I'm always going to miss her, too."

"But is that going to be okay, if I always miss her and I'm with you?"

"Yes, Max. That is okay. Will it be okay for you?"

"If what?"

"If I miss her, too, but let her go?"

"Yes," I said.

We turned the movie off. We turned the lights out. We went to sleep.

Chapter 9: Mentors

May 2020

Life with Megan was pleasant, but our plans changed immediately as Covid-19 ran through NYC and stopped life until it was almost non-existent. Megan's acting trip got canceled and she moved in full time with me. We did Zoom meetings with family and friends and cooked often. Megan showed me all of her favorite films, especially the ones that inspired her to act. Sometimes we stayed up late and woke up early, and other times, we went to bed early but woke up late. We watched re-runs of old basketball games and bet on the final score as if we couldn't search the outcome on our smartphones.

About a few months into the pandemic, Azra got engaged. I remember when Megan showed me the post on Instagram. I was blocked from Azra's account, and she was blocked from mine. But, if anything, the suspense was built up even more because Megan always showed me everything.

"She doesn't really look that happy, does she?" Megan asked as she showed me the post.

The way she held her iPhone by the left and right corners of the screen made it seem like she was showing me a super rare Topps rookie baseball card. I zoomed in on the photo collage. Azra wasn't even smiling as Yusef put the very bland and mediocre diamond onto her ring finger. I admittedly pictured myself getting down on one knee, imagined how I would have done it. Megan was not dumb, and she could see right through me.

"Okay, that's enough. Want to watch the news?"

"You say it like it's so exciting?"

"Well, it's better than nothing."

"Sure, turn it on."

After hours of social media, unfiltered news, reading and researching trends within the stock market and the cryptocurrency community, I began to overthink what exactly it was I was doing. It was then when it hit me: if Megan was going to be a part of my life, I needed to do what was going to make me happy long term.

"Where are you going?" Megan asked as I got up and made my way towards the door.

I picked up a fresh new medical mask that was resting on the table outside the entrance to my apartment.

"To clear my mind. To get a coffee. But Megan, I think when I come back inside, I'm going to know what I want to do. Actually, you know what, I'm just going to tell you now."

"Wait, slow down. You work in finance, you lost your job due to all the chaos. You'll be fine. You're okay, Max, don't rush it."

"Okay, well, I've had this idea for months now. I want to start a trading podcast. But not just any typical trading podcast. Like an actual business. And I've already thought about it; I can stream in the morning when the opening bell rings."

"Okay, just slow down."

I didn't listen to Megan's demands. "I could even hire an intern to run social media and handle marketing campaigns."

"Whoa, sounds like you thought this through. But I'm not sure if you want to toss away the career that you put a whole decade into just for some random idea?"

"Random idea?"

"I didn't mean it like that."

"Well, it sure sounded like you did."

"No, it's just that I'm being selfish because I don't have a fancy degree. I guess I'm just nervous, that's all."

"Megan, with all due respect, I can't let that decision sway me. Look, you're a talented actress, and when things open back up in the restaurant industry, I know you'll get back into your routine. But what about me? I have to take a risk sooner or later."

"Okay, yeah, I think you should go for it, what am I saying? I should be more supportive."

"Yeah, it sounds good, right?"

"Yeah, I have a friend who just invested in a few floors of shared spaces in Soho."

"Yeah, it's called a WeWork," I sarcastically replied.

"I know what a WeWork is," Megan defended herself.

I had to admit it, she brought a lot to the table, Megan had an enormous network.

"Send me the contact information and I'll reach out."

"Hey, I'm proud of you," Megan said.

"You're proud of me?" I grabbed Megan and began to kiss her neck.

"Max, stop, I thought you said you were heading out?"

"I was but now something else is on my mind."

"You're crazy," Megan said. "But I like it."

Megan brought out a different side of me.

My phone began to vibrate, it was my Human Resources Director at Braxen Capital. "This is Melissa, calling for Max."

Melissa, who also served as Colt's executive assistant, had only called me once, when I took off for five days for a cousin's bachelor party.

"Hey, Melissa," I said.

The other party went silent, but I could still hear static on the line. "Max, are you alone?"

Megan looked at me and made funny faces to get me to laugh, but I waved her off. "I'm not, but I can be."

"Please, if you can, Max."

I knew it was serious; Melissa was always a glass half full employee, never a bad attitude once, in all the years I worked with her. I told Megan to be quiet, if not with my voice, with my hands. She listened as the mood shifted.

"Yeah, I'm alone. What's up?" I walked into the bathroom and closed the door. My bathroom carried a modern luxury, but there was nothing large about it.

"It's about Colt," Melissa informed me.

I sat down on the toilet. The white crisp seat was just cleaned, and I could see my eyes as I looked down and remained quiet on the line.

"Just tell me. What happened?"

"It's his heart. He's not going to make it. It's Covid"

I fell to the floor. My elbow slammed on the toilet seat. I held the phone away from my ear. My life was shattered, broken into a thousand pieces.

"Are you there?"

I was seconds away from breaking down and crying, but I held it together. Somehow, someway.

"Max, I'm here. And I know you had some differences, but I know how close you two were."

"Yeah," I said. Tears begin to roll down my face.

"I know this is extremely difficult, and given the circumstances, there won't be any memorial service or even a private viewing."

"So, what should I do?"

"Well, there's something he bought for you when you finished graduate school. I remember he was too embarrassed to give it to you then, something about you getting the same one from your dad."

I looked down on the hands that ticked as I endured probably the hardest conversation of my life. The situation with Azra seemed silly, even trivial now. My Rolex watch was a gift I received from my father.

"What was it?" I asked.

"He bought you a Rolex, but I remember he was too embarrassed to deliver it to you. He engraved it as well."

"What did it say?"

"It said, *Max Yates, MBA.*"

"It said that?"

"It did, and I can mail it to you. That's another thing I wanted to go over. Is your address on file up to date?"

"Yeah, thanks, Melissa."

"Okay, well, then, if that's it. Stay safe, Max."

I hung up the phone and Megan walked into the bathroom while I lay there, my neck lodged up against the pearly white fixture.

"Max, is everything okay?"

"No, my boss isn't going to make it. He's going to die from the coronavirus."

Megan held me as I cried in her arms. I didn't know what to say so I just said, "No," on repeat.

"No," I yelled as it echoed throughout the room.

Megan ran her fingers through my hair.

"I will hold you," she said.

I never knew why she chose the words, but I'm glad she did.

Chapter 10: Time Goes On
March 2023

A few years went by, and the pandemic started to fade out. The government figured out a way to secure vaccines, although everyone still wore masks and received additional boosts of the same shot to avoid repeating the same mistake. Oh yeah, and they figured out a way to get more than half the country vaccinated and back to work.

Megan had reached out to her old friend from an acting class whose husband ran a small commercial leasing firm. I got a tiny cozy box office that overlooked Broadway right on the border of Chinatown, right on the corner of Soho, where the foot traffic started to pick up. It had everything—a shared lobby, ping pong tables outside the conference rooms with movie theater popcorn, and fountain soda. What else could a kid in a grown man's body ask for?

It was now 2023. The pandemic was still in the rearview but it certainly wasn't over… I don't think it ever will be. But still, I had moved on.

That day started out normal. I scanned my vaccination card against the side entrance and the doors opened. The security guards at the desk all wore black face masks, perhaps to be extra safe as normalcy began to flirt with New York City for the first time in what felt like ten years. I walked into my office, which was small yet cozy. I had framed the Forbes article that I was fortunate enough to have written up about me and my brand. "How a twenty-something-year-old turned a finance background into a brand of day trading, meet Colt Day Trading."

Yes, I named my company after my old boss. It was corny, but it felt right. I had a podcast, an Instagram account, and I suppose I developed an incredible following, thanks to lockdown. For the most part, I was all alone. I had guests that were pioneers in the industry, whether it be crypto enthusiasts, blockchain bloggers, or penny stock tweeters that wouldn't sleep until they pumped every last cent out of a newly launched company. Yet, for me, the rush came from being my own boss and ultimately starting my own legacy. Fridays were office optional for me, but, for some reason, I decided to go in. All my equipment was in the office, and I think it just made the day more enjoyable.

It was business as usual until a call came up from the front desk, "Hey, Max, you have a visitor!"

"Okay send 'em up" I didn't ask for a name, I just assumed it was someone I knew who had read my Forbes article. That was the only logical explanation.

And then, just like that, I saw the same woman who I had been with ten plus years prior, who I had chased after in a different country. Again, it was Azra.

"What are you doing here?" I asked.

"I read your article and Google searched you. I found the address to your office, and I just figured, what the hell, right?"

"You could have at least given me some time to fix this place up."

"No, I love it, it's amazing if I'm being honest."

I looked over at Azra once more. She had lost a lot of weight. She didn't look unhealthy, but she was close to it, but because she was a physician, she got a pass.

"Well, let me at least get you a water or a soda?"

"No, no I'm fine, just had an iced coffee before I stopped by."

I also had realized there was no ring on Azra's finger. It piqued my interest.

"So," I said as I leaned back on a computer chair that had seen decades of better days. "What's up?"

Azra's voice turned to grey. "I've just been thinking of you. Just a lot." Azra's voice went somber. "And I miss you, and I'm no longer with Yusef. He's back in Turkey."

"Wait, slow down?"

"Yeah, Max, it's fine, it's just been a lot. Could we maybe go for a walk and get a coffee? Talk more?"

I then thought about Colt and when he started and the story he had told me— the morning of 9/11 and the awful attacks and how his coffee was his second chance.

181

It was like Colt was still with me in my most pressured moments.

"Yeah, Azra, we can do that, just hold on. I need to shut off the Covid alarm when we exit and grab my coat. Deal? Just wait here."

I went to the side room where all leaseholders held their coats and jackets. I picked mine up and disabled the alarm so we could exit without issue. But, as I began to make my way towards Azra, I realized the pressure I would take on if I went down this all-familiar road.

Azra grew restless and she exited my office. The door was on auto-lock, and you couldn't enter back in unless you had the key in my pocket. If I left right now, I wouldn't have to see Azra again. I could escape her for good and she would receive the message once and for all. So, instead of going back to get Azra, I clicked the down arrow elevator key ten times fast. It reminded me of the same night Azra came and it brought me back to the moment I chased after her and how sorry I felt for my younger, immature, less intelligent self. The elevator came, I got in, and I exited the office building and headed home on the subway.

I had left Azra stranded, locked out of my office. A side of me felt guilty, while another part of me felt liberated and free from Azra. Yet, the thought of Azra's pain haunted me. As I rode the subway, I wondered if she was in danger or how she had been. I may not have been in love with

Azra anymore, but my heart still craved her, my soul was still curious of where Azra had gone.

I walked back into my apartment and Megan was there to give me a big hug. The apartment smelled amazing. There was NBA basketball on the big screen and a fresh pie of our favorite local pizza on the counter. She poured me a glass of Pepsi with extra ice cubes, and she served herself a tiny, yet full glass of red wine. My Fridays were way different now, I hardly visited the clubs, and when I did, it was to celebrate an old friend or catch up with a former classmate. Strictly networking. Yet what I had done to Azra just a few hours prior felt wrong.

"So, how was your Friday?" Megan smiled as cleaned forks and knives and stacked the glass of wine and soda side by side. She wore these cute purple gloves—completely excessive, but like I said, as cute as anything.

"It was great, how about yours?"

"Quiet, but good," Megan added. "Don't worry, auditions will pick up again soon. Plus, you're doing great with all these remote gigs. You're crushing it."

"Thanks, Max, that means a lot."

"So, I saw Azra today."

Megan stopped the dishes and threw her purple gloves into the sink. "What?"

"I saw Azra. She came to my office. I continued scrubbing. The cold water on my knuckles was as cold as Megan's reaction.

"You saw Azra today, and you're just telling me now after we ate dinner?"

"I don't see the big deal. Didn't we already discuss this years ago?"

"You don't see the big deal? Well, I do, because I still follow her on Instagram, and I know that she's single now. She and her fiancé broke up."

"I didn't know that."

"Oh, you didn't know that? Probably because you two are so immature that you're both blocked on each other's pages, and you know what that tells me?"

"What does that tell you?" I asked. Of course, I knew the answer, but the drama became a rush for me, something that got me off, it was unhealthy, but it was true.

"It tells me that at least one person is still in love with the other."

"Oh, come on, Megan!" I shouted. "You think I would have you living here in this studio apartment if I was still in love with Azra?"

"You say it like it's such a bad thing. I'm sorry that I took over your apartment. I want a bigger apartment."

"Well, we only have one true income right now, and that's fine, but this is all we can afford. Plus with prices now, it's not even worth looking."

"So now I'm the bad girl because I'm pursuing my dreams, just like you did?"

"No, you're not a bad person but you're making me feel guilty when I basically pay for everything. I do everything for you, I pay for your travel and your subway every month, and I don't mind but—"

"Sounds like you do, it sounds like you're holding it over my head."

"What would you say if I got coffee with Azra?"

"Did you get coffee with Azra today?"

"No, I didn't," I told Megan. "I didn't get coffee with Azra because I knew that would make you upset."

"I do not trust Azra, Max. What is so hard to understand? It is time for all of us to move on from her. She's like this leach. She takes and she takes, and she takes again."

Megan then left the kitchen and began to change into her pajamas in front of me. Megan was gorgeous, but often her temper overshadowed her natural beauty.

"Oh, don't be dramatic. She's a doctor, I'm sure she could afford her own way for travel and subway."

"Fuck you, Max, you're an asshole. What did you even see in her, she never loved you like I..." Megan cut herself off.

"What?"

"As I love you," Megan said. She walked back towards me to give me a hug. "I don't want to fight. You're right, you have every right to catch up with her, and I should be more respectful of that. You two dated for a long time, and I have to understand that and be respectful."

"Come here," I told Megan. I held her and kissed her on the forehead. "I love you. I'm sorry for being immature. You are right, it's time to move on from Azra."

"I'm just tired. Can we lay down and go to bed early tonight?" Megan begged.

"Yeah, of course, anything."

We laid down next to each other. Megan began to kiss my neck and I was ready to go. She continued to kiss me and made her way down my body. I wouldn't call it make-up sex, but it was above average lovemaking, Megan always knew how to calm me down.

"That was amazing, as usual," Megan said as she ran her fingers on my lips and over my nostrils. "You're the best ever."

"You're the best ever," I mimicked her.

Megan stood up with the covers over her chest, just like you see in the movies.

I was a lucky man to have Megan. Her love, affection, and passion were something I had taken for granted. But I finally understood it.

"I'm heading to bed. I'm sorry, Max, I'm exhausted."

"Okay, I'll probably be up for hours. I can just tell it's going to be one of those nights. By the way, do we have any more bottled water next to the nightstand?"

We were too lazy to put the bottle of water into the fridge, so instead, we kept it next to the nightstand in our partitioned bedroom.

"No, we're out, baby, grab a glass from the kitchen and use the ice and the faucet."

I was upset. I didn't like to use the faucet before bed, I liked to be hydrated. But I got up and made my way to the kitchen, (which was only fifteen feet away), and stared at the same glass that was next to Azra the early morning she left. It was the only clean one left. I analyzed the glass and examined its every edge and detail. I went into the freezer and took a couple of ice cubes and laid them at the bottom. They fell to the base and layered on top of one another. I quickly poured the water on the cubes as I gripped the glass tight. The liquid released like a frozen rope and made a crisp sound like a *sizzle* from fresh cooked food. I gulped the water fast and my thirst asked for more. So, I filled the glass back up as memories from my past encapsulated the cylinder.

I walked back to bed and put the glass next to me. I tossed and turned for a few hours, and eventually, my eyes faded in and out of consciousness. The television was still on, and the late-night news played on repeat. I was in and out, out and in, and I rolled over towards Megan, but she was deep into her sleep, and I couldn't hold her, so like nights in my past, I was all alone again. Then, as my reality started to fade, I began to dream. I was half asleep and torn between what was real and what was a dream. My thoughts began to take over and I started to wander into the world of sleep. The news played in the background, "A medical doctor who fought Covid-19 was found dead in her NYC apartment. A recent fight with her boyfriend, who is attending NYU Law School, was observed by neighbors shortly before the crime was reported." Then a photo of Azra appeared. It was the same picture they used for her freshman soccer roster. The news story followed. "Azra was only twenty-nine years old."

But because of these thoughts, I began to think of Azra at my office, and I wondered if I was responsible for her death. Would I be the next suspect on the news? Was I a criminal trapped in the body of a preppy finance professional from the mid-Atlantic? These thoughts and fears overtook my heart, and I woke up aggressively trying to catch my breath as my blood pumped fast and my throat swallowed.

"Max, are you okay?" Megan asked. "What's wrong?"

I had imagined the entire scenario, but it was just a dream—a nightmare, I suppose. I caught my breath. Azra was fine, at least my thoughts weren't aligned with what was taking place in the real world.

"Just a bad dream, I'm okay, go back to bed."

"Take a drink, it's on the side of your bed."

This time, the ice had melted, the liquid crawled on the side of the glass like demons and angels battling for a seat in heaven only to have fallen to the depths of hell in pursuit of eternal freedom. I took a sip; it was no longer a glass that

I feared but rather an old reminder that I embraced. It seemed like no matter how much I drank, the water wouldn't go away. So, I placed it back on the nightstand next to the light. I caught my breath and held Megan tight.

I looked at the glass one last time. It was beautiful, but now it was time for me to turn off the light and go to bed. I closed my eyes and smiled— I had let the past evaporate with time. And, finally, for the first time ever, I had moved forward, and stopped chasing.

Made in United States
North Haven, CT
15 July 2022

21433870R00125